Worth the Trip

Other books by Tara Sivec

Romantic Comedy

The Chocolate Lovers Series:
Seduction and Snacks (Chocolate Lovers #1)
Futures and Frosting (Chocolate Lovers #2)
Troubles and Treats (Chocolate Lovers #3)

The Chocoholics Series:
Love and Lists (Chocoholics #1)
Passion and Ponies (Chocoholics #2)
Tattoos and TaTas (Chocoholics #2.5)

Romantic Suspense

The Playing With Fire Series:
A Beautiful Lie (Playing With Fire #1)
Because of You (Playing With Fire #2)
Worn Me Down (Playing With Fire #3)
Closer to the Edge (Playing With Fire #4)

Romantic Suspense/Erotica

The Ignite Trilogy:
Burned (Ignite Trilogy Volume 1)
Branded (Ignite Trilogy Volume 2)

New Adult Drama
Watch Over Me

Romantic Comedy/Mystery

The Fool Me Once Series:
Shame on You (Fool Me Once #1)
Shame on Me (Fool Me Once #2)
Shame on Him (Fool Me Once #3)

Contemporary Romance
Fisher's Light

Worth the Trip

(A Fisher's Light Companion Novella)

By
Tara Sivec

Worth the Trip
Copyright © 2015 Tara Sivec
Print Edition

All rights reserved. No part of this book may be reproduced or transmitted in any form or by any means, electronic or mechanical, including photocopying, recording or by any information storage and retrieval system without written permission from the author, except for the inclusion of brief quotations in a review. The characters and events portrayed in this book are fictitious. Any similarity to real persons, living or dead is coincidental and not intended by the author.

Disclaimer
This is a work of adult fiction. The author does not endorse or condone any of the behavior enclosed within. The subject matter is not appropriate for minors. Please note this novel contains profanity and explicit sexual situations. All trademarks and copyrighted items mentioned are the property of their respective owners.

Editing by Nikki Rushbrook

Cover Design by Indie Book Cover Designs
www.michellepreast.com

Interior Design by Paul Salvette, BB eBooks
bbebooksthailand.com

Prologue

AGE IS JUST a number.

That's what people say, at least. Sitting here on my old, worn-out couch, flipping through a photo album in the middle of the night, I think those people are full of shit. I have two hundred Canadian coins in a tin on my bookshelf. There are sixty-one pictures in this photo album. I have one hundred and four old 45's that I still listen to on my 1953 RCA record player. *Those* are just numbers, the sum total of *things* that I've collected over the years.

As I turn the page in the photo album resting on my lap, I see the age spots and wrinkles on the top of my hand. I feel the arthritis in my right hip and knee flaring up because I've been sitting on this couch too long. When I look in the mirror, I don't see a good-looking, cocky son-of-a-bitch who had life by the balls, I see an old man with too many regrets and I feel each and every moment of my eighty-three years.

Age isn't just a number. It's days, weeks,

months, *years* of disappointments and memories and watching your life pass right in front of your eyes, knowing you can't go back and do things differently. You have one shot to get it right and if you screw it up…well, that's just too damn bad.

I glance over at the grandfather clock, standing tall next to the couch, ticking loudly in the quiet room. Staring at the pendulum swinging back and forth, with the heavy weight of the photo album filled with memories of my time here on this earth in my lap, feels like I'm watching the hands of time count down to the end of my life.

So many years on this island, taking care of neighbors and friends and making sure my son never screwed up his own son the way I did him. Years of living, but not really being alive. My son grew into a man I hardly recognize and has made choices I don't agree with, but how can I blame him? My actions were the catalyst for the path he chose. My grandson is fighting his way back to the woman he loves, and while I'm happy that he's finally removed his head from his ass where she's concerned, I realize that everyone around me has their own lives to live and all I have left is this book full of memories. I've never regretted being alone all these years. I think about her smile and her kisses that still haunt my dreams and I'm certain that no other woman would have ever compared to the one I married.

I run my fingertips over the face that fills so many pictures in this album. The woman who loved me more than I ever deserved. The woman who made me feel like I could do anything I put my mind to. She loved me until her dying breath and it's only fair that I do the same.

A sharp pain shoots up my left arm and my hand starts to tingle. Flexing my hand, I shake my arm to try and get it to stop. It's been doing this off and on since I woke up and I know I should probably call Doc Wilson, but I've got more important things to attend to. My time on this earth is coming to an end, and I've gotten my affairs in order and done what I can to push my grandson back into the arms of the woman he loves so that I can die knowing he's going to be okay. I wish I could fix the mess I made with my son, but some mistakes can't be mended with an apology. There isn't a Band-Aid big enough to stop the bleeding in that wound. I can't even tell him that I did the best I could, because Lord knows that's a damn lie.

Gently peeling back the thin sheet of plastic covering the photos in the album, I pull out the first black and white photo and smile to myself, even though seeing her so young and vibrant and full of life makes me feel like someone shoved a knife right through my heart. I grab the notebook and pen sitting next to me on the couch and start writing. I know I'm a coward for waiting this long to explain my side of things, but it's time I told my story.

I should have tried long before now to make amends. There's nothing like staring right at death's door to put a fire under your ass. I'm going to die with enough regrets to fill ten notebooks and that's a tough pill to swallow, but when I meet my maker, I want to be able to hold my head high with the knowledge that at least I confronted all my mistakes.

The Life and Times of Jefferson "Trip" Fisher
I'm sorry, I love you, please forgive me.

Chapter 1

June 1939

"COME ON, JUST dump it over your head. Don't be a chicken!"

Beverly scrunches up her face and gets angry when I call her that. She HATES being called a chicken.

"I am NOT a chicken, Jefferson Fisher!" she argues, holding the bucket of sand in her arms and looking down at her dress. "My mom just bought me this dress. I can't get it dirty."

I stare at the stupid blue dress, snatch the bucket from her arms and dump it over my own head, laughing as the sand rains down on top of me. I scoop more sand into the bucket and hand it back to Beverly. If I have to babysit a dumb girl, then I'm going to have some fun. My parents and her parents are good friends and I have to spend every weekend with her, making sure she doesn't get her silly dress dirty or get hurt just because I'm two years older than her and have to be in charge.

"See? I'm not dirty. Now it's your turn. If you don't do it, I'm going to tell everyone that Beverly Ann O'Byrne is a chicken!"

I start making clucking noises and Beverly finally huffs, takes the bucket from my hands and dumps it over her own head. I realize a little too late that I filled up the bucket with wet sand, not dry like I used. Instead of raining down on top of her head, it plops there, sticking in her hair and dripping down into her eyes.

Beverly starts howling and yelling at me, trying to wipe the wet mush out of her eyes, but she just makes it worse, spreading it all over her face. I'm laughing so hard that my side starts to ache, and I clutch it as I close my eyes and continue chuckling. Something wet smacks me in the face, cutting off my laughter, and my eyes pop open. No longer angry, Beverly has a huge smile on her face and before I can call her a dumb ninny, she scoops up a handful of wet sand and throws it right at my chest. I stare down in shock as the sand plops from my chest into my lap.

"Oh, you're in big trouble now!" I tell her as I grab two handfuls of sand and throw them, hitting her right in the chest, as well.

WORTH THE TRIP

We quickly scramble away from each other, scooping up sand with our muddy hands and pelting the piles back and forth until we collapse into a laughing, dirty mess.

"Beverly Ann! Look how dirty your dress is!"

We stop immediately and stare guiltily at the man standing a few feet from us, his hands on his hips and a scowl on his face.

"And Mister Jefferson," he says, turning his face to mine. "Are you the reason my daughter is filthy this morning?"

I see a hint of a smile behind his frown and I jump up from the sand and walk over to him.

"It wasn't my idea, it was Beverly's. She wanted to play in the sand, but I tried to tell her not to get dirty."

Beverly jumps up and runs over to us. "He's lying, Daddy! It was his idea!"

Mr. O'Byrne throws his head back and laughs before grabbing both of our dirty hands and walking us up towards the house.

"What am I going to do with you two? We're supposed to be having a nice breakfast and now look at you. I'm going to have to hose you two off with the garden hose!"

Beverly and I look up at him, horrified.

7

"No! That water is so cold!" she protests.

"How about I just throw you in the ocean to wash you off?" her father suggests with another laugh when we give him a dirty look.

"Daddy!" Beverly complains.

He scoops her up into his arms, not even caring that he's getting sand all over himself. "Okay, fine. I guess we'll just go inside and tell your mother a huge sand monster came along and attacked both of you."

I nod my head emphatically as Mr. O'Byrne situates Beverly in his arms and reaches for my hand again. "Yes! It was a big, dirty sand monster and he just started throwing his dirty sand all over us! We tried to fight back, but it was no use."

We all laugh as we continue on into the house for breakfast with my parents and Beverly's parents, something we've done every weekend for as long as I can remember. The story of the sand monster gets bigger and better as we walk and I KNOW our mothers are going to believe it.

We walk through the back door and Mr. O'Byrne sets Beverly down next to me. "You two stay here, I'll head into the dining room and plead your case to your mothers."

He ruffles my hair and gives Beverly a kiss

on the cheek before turning and walking away, leaving us alone by the door.

Beverly looks at me and I look at her.

"If my mom doesn't believe my dad about the sand monster, I'm telling her it was all your fault," she informs me, crossing her arms in front of her.

"Oh, yeah? Well, I'm going to tell MY mom that you threw sand at me first. You started it," I reply, crossing my own arms and glaring at her.

We stand toe-to-toe, shooting dirty looks at each other while we listen to low, murmured voices in the other room, waiting for one of our mothers to start shouting at us.

"At least I wasn't a chicken," Beverly informs me, lifting her chin high.

"You're still a chicken," I remind her, adding a few squawks and a flap of my arms.

"BEVERLY O'BYRNE AND JEFFERSON FISHER! GET IN HERE RIGHT NOW!"

We drop our arms to our sides and stare down the hall towards the dining room.

"Uh-oh," I mutter under my breath.

"Race you to the lighthouse?" Beverly whispers.

She turns, throws open the back door and

takes off running. With one last look over my shoulder, I follow behind her, back onto the beach. I'd rather get a whoopin' for running away than listen to our mothers yell at us for getting dirty. Plus, I can't keep letting a *girl* beat me to the lighthouse. One of these days, I'm going to catch her.

Chapter 2

SMILING TO MYSELF and ignoring the pain in my chest and arm that is getting steadily worse, I put the photo of Beverly when she was five and me at seven, covered in sand from head-to-toe, back into the photo album and smooth the protective plastic over top of it. Even though she was covered in sand, she is smiling the biggest smile in the world at the camera. Her long, curly brown hair is in disarray and I can just hear her mother shouting at her to run a brush through it after we finally made our way back to the house an hour later because we were hungry.

Beverly and I were always trying to get each other in trouble and one-up each other. I was only two years old when Beverly's father moved his family to the island to open an accounting firm. My dad, a fisherman turned financier, sought out Mr. O'Bryne for advice on how to navigate the stock market and the two became fast friends. Our mothers bonded over talk of babies and the rest, as they say, is history. The friendship grew when my father opened Fisher's Bank and Trust in 1940, and impressed with the way Mr. O'Byrne managed the books of the thriving local businesses, hired him as his bank manager.

Our parents being the best of friends, Beverly and I were frequently thrown together, and I resented having a girl tagging along after me all the time. I didn't want my friends thinking I'd rather play with a girl than with them and I remember being embarrassed that she was always following me around. Two years younger than me, Bevy was just an annoying little baby who couldn't do anything for herself and I hated always being left in charge of her.

Make sure Beverly doesn't go near the water.

Make sure Beverly doesn't fall and hurt herself.

If I had a nickel for every time I heard one of those requests, I'd be a rich man.

I can still recall the exact moment Bevy became more than the irritating little brat who followed me around all the time, the day I began looking at her with a little more respect and found myself actually WANTING to hang around her.

Closing my eyes, I rest my head on the back of the couch and try to ignore how much worse the pain in my chest is getting. I think back to the spring of 1940, the year our lives began to change. I can still feel the wind in my hair as I raced down Main Street, my whole life before me and not a care in the world, and I think about Beverly. Sweet, little six-year-old Beverly, who put me in my place and never ceased to amaze me.

Chapter 3

April 1940

"WELL, WHAT DO you think, son? JEFFERSON!"

My father's booming voice makes me jump and I turn away from the window that looks out on Main Street, trying not to look guilty.

"Um, it's a building," I reply in a bored voice, my eyes darting back to the window when I hear my friends run by, whooping and hollering as they chase each other.

"This isn't just any building, Jefferson, this is Fisher's Bank and Trust. It's your future and your legacy. Do you have any idea how hard I've worked to make this happen for you?" he lectures.

I try not to sigh, but it's the first nice day of spring and I want to be outside with my friends, not in some dumb building filled with desks and ledgers and not enough sunlight. I see my friend Billy stop in front of the big window next to the door and watch as he presses his mouth to the glass and blows until his cheeks are as big as baseballs. I laugh loudly and my father grumbles under his breath, walking around me until he's blocking my view before squatting down in front of me and giving me a stern look.

"I know you'd rather be outside, son, but this is important. The bank will be open in just a few weeks and it's going to be a very important business on this island. It's exciting and it will change our entire lives," he explains.

I don't know why he's making such a big deal about this. I like our life just the way it is. Well, I liked it before my father spent all his time here in this stupid bank, back when he was home for supper and played catch with me down by the beach. When my father was still a fisherman, I got to ride on the boat with him all the time. It was quiet and peaceful and we spent all of our time talking about Joe DiMaggio, our favorite baseball player, instead of money and loans and other boring things I don't care about. DiMaggio is the greatest baseball player in the world, but Dad doesn't have time to talk about him anymore. He's down at this bank all the time and when I try to talk to him, he always shushes me because he's busy counting something or other.

The bell above the front door chimes and we turn our heads to see Mr. O'Byrne and Beverly walk through the door. I grumble under my breath because I really thought I'd get to play with my friends today without being stuck with HER.

"Jefferson, Mr. O'Byrne is going to be the new bank manager here at Fisher's Bank and Trust, isn't that wonderful?"

I shrug as Mr. O'Byrne looks down at me. "Just think, Jefferson, some day YOU'RE going to own this bank and then YOU'LL be my boss!"

Mr. O'Byrne and my father share a laugh. I don't like how the two of them are staring at me. I don't like being cooped up in this building and I don't want to talk about getting older anymore. I like being eight just fine.

"Can I go outside now, sir?" I beg.

My father shakes his head at me while Mr. O'Byrne laughs again.

"Go on, go play. Mr. O'Byrne and I have some business to discuss. Why don't you take Beverly with you?"

I knew it was coming, but it still makes

me angry. Why do I have to take her with me everywhere I go? Doesn't she have her own friends? She needs to go play with dolls all day, not hang out with us guys while we do guy stuff. My friends aren't going to want to play with a *girl*.

I start to argue, but I hold back, not wanting to be sent to bed without supper tonight. My mom is making meatloaf and I'm not about to miss that because of some stupid girl.

Turning away from the adults, I stomp towards the door, not even caring whether or not she's following me. As soon as I get outside, the sun hits my face and I take a deep breath of the salty ocean air.

I hear a sigh next to me and I look over to find Beverly standing on the sidewalk with her eyes closed and her face turned towards the sun.

"TRIP! Come on! We're going to climb the trees behind Barney's!" Billy shouts from the other side of the street.

"Climb trees? I love to climb trees!" Beverly states excitedly. "Why did he call you Trip?"

I stare longingly at Billy as he races off down Main Street. "It's my nickname. It's dumb. YOU like to climb trees? But you're a girl. And you're wearing a *dress*."

She shrugs. "Just because I'm a girl doesn't mean I can't do the same things boys can do. Why is your nickname Trip?"

I don't want to talk about my stupid nickname. I want to know more about the boy-things she thinks she can do, but she's staring at me with these big blue eyes like a little puppy, so I give in.

"We were running races a few weeks ago and I fell a couple of times. The guys started calling me Trip and it just sort of stuck," I tell her.

"Well, I think it's neat. I don't have a nickname. How come you've never given me a nickname?" she asks.

I roll my eyes and crane my neck to see Billy and the guys disappear around the corner down the street.

"Fine, I'll give you a nickname if you'll stop bugging me. We call my friend Billy, Kid because he wants to be a gun-toting outlaw like Billy the Kid," I tell her. "Since your name is Beverly, how about Bevy?"

Her eyes widen and a smile lights up her face. She looks at me like I'm the best person in the entire world and it makes my heart beat almost as fast as when Billy and I race.

She clasps her hands together under her chin and sighs. "I love it. I love it so much. Bevy is a great nickname! Will you call me that all the time?"

I shrug distractedly. "Sure, Bevy. Whatever you want."

She giggles and then takes off running across the street, shouting over her shoulder as she goes. "My brother taught me how to be the best tree climber in the entire world. He also taught me how to be the best rock skipper, kick the canner and hide and seeker."

I run to catch up with her as she makes it across the street and starts skipping, not believing a word she says. She's never climbed one tree in all the years I've known her. She plays with dolls and has tea parties and other stupid, boring things. Her brother Benjamin is A LOT older than us, so old that he has facial hair and everything. I heard my mom say that Bevy was an "oops baby," whatever that means. I think it means that when she was born, her parents said, "Oops! We'd rather have a boy, not a girl, because girls are dumb!"

Benjamin just turned twenty-one, which is really old, and because of that, he had to go be a sailor in the Navy. I still don't think he taught her how to do any of those things she said, even if he is the coolest guy in the world and showed me how to whittle wood last summer.

"There's no way you're the best tree climber," I inform her.

Even if she runs faster than all the boys on the island, I've been climbing trees since I could walk, and I consider myself an expert on the subject.

She stops in the middle of the sidewalk, puts her hands on her hips and glares at me.

"I'll bet you my marble collection that I'm a better tree climber than *you*."

I laugh right in her face and take off running. She immediately follows, her feet pounding on the sidewalk, and I'm not surprised when she catches right up to me.

"Don't you laugh at me, Trip Fisher! I'll show you just how much better I am at ALL of those things!" she argues as I push my legs harder and faster and we race our way through town.

"You can't call me Trip! Only my friends can call me Trip!" I shout back in irritation.

By the time we get to the cropping of trees behind Barney's, my lungs feel like they're going to explode and sweat is dripping down my face. Beverly beats me by a few inches and I'm a little surprised she doesn't make fun of me. If *I* were the winner, I would have rubbed it in her face, just like I do whenever I beat her at something, which I'm sad to say, isn't very often. For some reason, I'm not angry that a girl ran faster than me and all my friends saw it. I'm proud. Billy and the rest of my friends watch in awe as she immediately starts climbing one of the biggest trees, crawling up into the branches with ease and leaving us standing around the base with our mouths open.

"Well, come on! Are you just going to stand there all day staring?!" she shouts down to us.

Everyone looks at me and I just shrug before grabbing onto the lowest branch and hauling myself up to follow her.

It was the first of MANY times that I would follow Bevy O'Byrne. There was something about her that made me want to follow her anywhere.

Chapter 4

BEVY CLIMBED THOSE damn trees with us all day, moving faster and going higher than any of us cocky little boys. My buddies took to her immediately and, after a while, didn't even realize she was a girl showing us all up. She wasn't afraid to play rough and she didn't shy away from doing scary and exciting things. She thrived on that crap and it made us all love her and want to be her friend.

Before that day, I ignored Bevy when my friends were around because I didn't want them to know I hung out with a girl all the time, even if I was forced to do it. After that day, I was proud to call her my friend and told her she could call me Trip just like the rest of my buddies. Bevy just had a way about her that made everyone want to be close to her. She made you laugh and she challenged you every step of the way. From that day on, Bevy and I did everything together. I was closer to her than almost anyone and she fit in with my group of guy friends like she had always been there.

Don't get me wrong, I still teased her all the time about the fancy dresses her mother made her wear and how her long, curly hair always looked like a complete disaster because of all the running and climbing she did. I remember making gagging noises every time my father told me that you tease the ones you love the most. At eight years old, girls were still gross–even Bevy.

Our families still did everything together at that point, but I didn't mind it so much any more, even if Bevy WAS better than me at everything. It wasn't until the following year that life as we knew it came to a crashing halt. Things changed for both of our families on that sad day, and nothing was ever the same.

As a child, you don't really grasp the magnitude of grief or know what it's like to have your whole world torn apart, but Beverly and her family made me understand. When tragedy struck, I immediately stopped teasing her and trying to get her in trouble all the time. I knew from that moment on, I would stick by her side and do whatever I could to make her smile.

Pulling the next photo out of the album, I run the tips of my fingers over the young faces of Bevy at seven and myself at nine. I'm wearing a suit with my hair combed neatly to the side and Bevy is surprisingly clean in her dark dress with a bow in her hair. We're sitting on chairs in the corner of my parent's home and while I look bored out of my mind, Bevy's face is clearly filled with grief. I can recall that day like it was yesterday. I remember feeling bad later on because I'd complained to my mother about being bored. I remember sitting on the beach, listening to Bevy tell me how her family was falling apart and how scared she was. I remember being so incredibly angry for the way Mr. and Mrs. O'Byrne treated the little girl that they should have loved more than anything, but pushed to the side.

My poor Bevy. I wish I could go back in time and wrap my arms around that little girl all over again and tell her everything would be okay.

Chapter 5

December 1941

"PLEASE CAN WE go outside, Mom? Please?" I beg, tugging on the bow tie I was forced to wear, wondering if I would be the first nine-year-old to die from strangulation after wearing this dumb thing all day.

"Pretty please, Mrs. Fisher? We promise we won't get dirty," Bevy adds, batting her eyelashes and smiling up at my mother.

That's all it takes for my mom to smile down at the two of us and shake her head in defeat. It's the first real smile Bevy has shown us in days and I know my mother would say yes to anything at this point. Maybe I should have Bevy ask her about that puppy I've been wanting…

"Bevy, did you ask your father if you could go outside?" My mother questions softly as she smiles and waves at someone behind us.

Bevy's older brother, Benjamin, was killed a few weeks ago. Bevy's parents were always so proud of him for joining the Navy. They talked about him all the time and when Benjamin wrote letters, we'd all gather around their dining room table so Mrs. O'Byrne could read them out loud. Benjamin had gotten a job on the mainland after he graduated high school, so he wasn't around that much before he joined the Navy, but he came home as often as he could to hang out with Bevy and me. He'd tell us stories about being older and how much fun he was having being out on his own. He was the neatest guy in the world, and I wanted to be just like him when I grew up.

He'd only been home once in the year since he'd left for the Navy, but seeing him in his crisp, white uniform and listening to him talk about his adventures at sea were the highlights of my young life.

A few weeks ago, we were having a late lunch at Bevy's house after church when the ballgame we were listening to on the radio was interrupted by an emergency broadcast. Navy ships stationed at Pearl Harbor were under attack. It was the start of a war. My mom cried and my dad held his head in his hands. Bevy's mom started screaming and crying while her dad raced around the house, making phone calls and trying to calm his wife. Bevy and I sat in shock at the table, not really understanding what was going on. It wasn't until a few days later that we found out Benjamin was aboard the *USS Arizona*, one of the ships that went down, and he would no longer be writing letters or coming home to tell us all about the exciting things he got to do as a sailor.

My parents had everyone from the memorial service come to our house afterwards so that Bevy's mom could rest. Bevy's dad had to practically carry her into the church before the service and again to the car afterwards. I didn't like how loudly she cried and wailed; it made me feel uncomfortable. Bevy sat quietly in the front pew all by herself through the entire memorial while her dad tended to her mom. I tried to make funny faces at her to get her to laugh, but it didn't work.

"My dad told me he was busy and not to bother him," Bevy says quietly as she stares down at her shoes.

My mom looks sadly at Bevy and runs her hand over her brown curls.

"Go on, get out of here, you two. Trip, if you ruin that new suit, you will be hanging up the laundry outside for the next month," she warns.

Bevy and I look at each other and smile before thanking my mom quickly and escaping out the door.

"Race you down Main Street! Last one to the lighthouse is a rotten egg!" Bevy shouts as she takes off faster, her laughter trailing behind her as I follow. It's so nice to hear her laugh that I don't even care if she beats me. We run as fast as we can through town, the streets nearly deserted because most of the island is huddled in my living room, paying their respects to the O'Byrne's. The streets are usually bustling with happy islanders making last minute Christmas purchases this time of year, but everyone has been in a panic since all the talk of war started. Instead of celebrating the holiday season, people are always crying and in place of the Christmas party my father throws for the residents of Fisher's Island, he's hosted a bunch of town meetings at the bank so that the mayor can calm them down. All of a sudden, Fisher's Island is a sad place to live and I hate it. I want to have fun and laugh and talk to people on the street, but everyone is always in a hurry and no one has anything nice to say. They argue and cry and they're all so scared. I don't really understand what they're afraid of, but my friends and I have been whittling guns out of tree branches so that we can do our part. We patrol the beach every day just in case the bad guys try to come *here*. I tried telling Mr. Geyser, the grocer, that my friends and I will keep everyone safe, but he just told me to scram. It feels good to be having fun and racing through town without the weight of the islanders' sadness and worry coming down on us.

We make it to the other end of the island in record time and, as usual, Bevy beats me. We collapse in a heap on the sand at the base of the lighthouse, staring up at the cloudless sky while we catch our breath.

"Hey, Bevy, can I ask you something?"

She pushes up from her back and spreads the skirt of her dress around her knees while I fold my hands behind my head and breathe in the salty ocean air.

"If you're going to ask me to let you win one of our races, the answer is still no."

I laugh at the stern look in her face and shake my head. "Well, that's not what I was gonna ask, but since you brought it up...."

Bevy grabs a handful of sand and tosses it at my chest. I sit up quickly, laughing as I brush the sand off of my new dress shirt.

"I'm just kidding!" I tell her with another laugh. "I wanted to ask you something serious."

She raises her eyebrows and waits for me to continue.

"How come you don't want to talk about Benjamin anymore?"

I know she's sad that her brother is gone, but she hasn't said one word about him all week. She doesn't even want to talk about the funny stories he used to tell us, even though I'm sure those would make her smile again. Whenever I say his name, she looks around all worried-like and tells me to be quiet.

Bevy immediately looks away from me and stares out at the ocean. She's quiet for so long that I think she's not going to answer me.

"Benjamin was the best big brother. When he came to the island every weekend, he taught me how to run fast and how to climb trees. Benjamin taught me everything I know," she tells me softly.

Her voice sounds so sad and I don't like it. I like it when Bevy smiles and when Bevy laughs because you can't help but join her. She's got the biggest smile and the greatest

WORTH THE TRIP

laugh. The only times I've ever seen her sad are the few times we've had to go to her house the past few weeks and I don't like it. I make sure to let her choose which game we play after that and I always take her to the candy store on Main Street and use my allowance to let her pick a piece of penny candy just so she'll be happy again, but it never works.

Bevy picks up a stick lying next to her and starts writing out letters with the end of it in the hard, packed sand. I watch her quietly for a few minutes until she finishes and notice she spelled out Benjamin.

"I'm never allowed to talk about Benjamin. If I say his name, it makes my dad angry and my mom cry, so I don't talk about him to anyone," she tells me as she stares at his name in the sand. "My parents loved him a lot. I think they loved him more than me. Remember when I skinned my knee the other day and it was bleeding?"

I nod my head quietly. Bevy and I climbed to the very top of the biggest tree behind Barney's and she slipped on the way down. She cried the whole way home.

"I went right into my parents' room and my mom yelled at me. She told me my crying gave her a headache. My dad heard her yelling and came running in. He told me to leave her alone and stop bothering her. My leg was bleeding really bad and they didn't care. They don't care about anything anymore but Benjamin being gone."

She sniffles and rubs the back of her hand under her nose.

"It's okay, Bevy. I still care. I'll fix you up the next time your leg is bleeding and you can talk about Benjamin whenever you want with me," I tell her quietly.

She cranes her neck and looks behind us at the lighthouse.

"Benjamin told me in his letters how much he missed the island. He said that sometimes, he'd be on his ship and look out over the water and imagine that he could see the light from the lighthouse and that he knew it would guide him home when it was time."

I turn around with her and we both stare at the revolving light at the top of the structure.

"I don't think we're even going to celebrate Christmas this year," she tells me sadly, looking away from the light and back out at the water. "I asked my dad yesterday if we could go get a Christmas tree and he told me to stop being so selfish. I just want my mom to see the sparkling lights on the tree because maybe it will make her happy again. Maybe she'll want to come out of her room and it will get her to stop crying all the time."

Today is the first time Mrs. O'Byrne has been out of her room in two weeks. I overheard my parents saying she's got something wrong with her heart, that it got broken or something. I don't know how someone breaks their heart. Maybe she was climbing too many trees and she fell. I've never had anyone I know die before. My grandparents and all my aunts and cousins are alive. Mrs. O'Byrne doesn't eat, she doesn't come to our house for dinner anymore and she doesn't talk to anyone. I'm really sad that I'll never hear Benjamin tell us great stories anymore, but I don't want to lock myself in my room forever. That would be boring.

I scoot closer to Bevy, lift my arm and hang it loosely around her shoulders, pulling her to my side. She leans her head down and rests it on my shoulder as we stare out at the setting sun and the seagulls swooping down to catch fish out of the ocean.

"You're not selfish at all, Bevy," I tell her quietly. "If you don't have Christmas at your house, you can come to our house. My mom will make us hot chocolate and I'll even let you open all of my presents."

Bevy sighs happily and we sit in silence for a long time, just watching the waves crash up onto the shore.

"Hey, Trip, can you promise me something?" she asks softly after a few minutes. "Promise me you'll never be a sailor and leave me."

My chest feels tight and my eyes start to burn. I immediately clear my throat and blink my eyes quickly because boys don't cry. I hate that this is happening to Bevy. I hate that she's so sad and her parents don't even care when she gets hurt. I would promise her anything she asked as long as it kept her from being sad.

Resting my chin on top of Bevy's head as the sun disappears over the horizon, I make her the promise I would keep for the rest of my life.

"I promise, Bevy," I whisper. "I'll never leave you."

Chapter 6

BEVY'S PARENTS NEVER recovered from the loss of Benjamin and they didn't speak about him from that point on. Bevy wasn't allowed to utter his name when she was at home, so I made sure she knew she could talk about Benjamin as often as she wanted with me.

It feels good to write all of this down for my family, to tell Jefferson about his mother as a young girl and to introduce Fisher to the great-uncle who was a hero just like him.

The very next photo in the album is of Benjamin in his uniform the day he shipped out to Hawaii on what would be his first and last assignment. At twenty-two years old, he had such a baby face and it's hard to fathom he and so many others aboard those ships in 1941 never came home to their families. Pearl Harbor really was a day that would live in infamy, and one that tore apart the O'Byrne family in such a way that nothing was ever able to put it back together.

From that day on, Bevy never again needed my help getting dirty and finding trouble. She did everything she could to get her parents' attention, from ruining brand new dresses to throwing a rock through their living room window. She thought the more heinous her crimes, the more likely it was that her mother would eventually come out of her bedroom and scold her. She stopped hanging around with other girls at school and stuck with my friends and me instead. She thought if she excelled at climbing trees and other boy things, her dad would love her as much as he did Benjamin, but all it did was make him angry when she came home dirty and torn up and he'd send her to her room without supper and make her stay there all alone. He never understood that Bevy acted out because she was tired of being alone. She just wanted someone to love her.

As the years dragged on, regardless of what Bevy did, her parents continued to pay very little attention her. Her mother never came out of her room again and Mr. O'Byrne spent all of his time working, ignoring the daughter who needed him so much.

For the next ten years, Bevy ate dinner at our house every night and went to church with us every Sunday. I was probably the most surprised out of everyone when Bevy joined the church choir with my mom. She had the best singing voice in the world and it wasn't long before she was given solos every Sunday.

It's almost like my parents adopted Bevy. My mom bought her play clothes and kept them at our house so Bevy wouldn't get in trouble when she got dirty after we horsed around outside. She even bought Bevy Christmas presents every single year and got Bevy her very own tiny Christmas tree for her bedroom so that she could enjoy the sparkling lights, since her father refused to celebrate anything anymore.

Bevy never wanted to spend time at her own house and really, I didn't blame her. The handful of times I'd run over there with her to get something or to pick her up so we could play, I didn't want to stay very long, either. The house was dark and damp inside since the curtains were always drawn. It wasn't a happy, noisy house like mine. My mom kept the curtains and windows wide open because she liked to hear the sounds of the ocean and the big radio in the living room was always playing music. Sometimes I'd walk into the living room and find my parents laughing and dancing to whatever song was playing.

Bevy said we had to whisper when we went inside *her* house because loud noises would make her mother angry and she hated when her mother got angry.

Bevy spent every waking moment at my house, and when she was grounded for one transgression or another, I would run over to her house, toss rocks at her bedroom window and help her sneak out. We spent a lot of time down by the lighthouse talking about Benjamin and what we wanted to be when we grew up. Until Benjamin's death, I always thought I wanted to be a soldier. I remember sitting on the floor in our living room, crowded around the radio with my parents, listening to the news reports about Pearl Harbor for weeks while my mother cried and my father got angry. It was all anyone talked about on Fisher's Island for a very long time. No one could believe we'd been attacked on our own soil and living on an island surrounded by the water made people nervous. I still remember my friends and I walking up and down the coast with our makeshift guns, standing guard in an effort to keep the island safe. I'm not sure what the hell a group of kids could have done if a bunch of planes flew overhead and dropped bombs on us, but it made us feel important. We were protecting our home the only way we knew how.

Setting the photo album, notepad and pen on the couch next to me, I push my old, tired body up and shuffle to the other side of the room to a framed picture hanging on the wall. I smile to myself, even though the photo fills me with great sadness, ignoring the sweat beading on my forehead and refusing to go back to bed. This photo was one of my mother's favorites and she had it framed for Bevy when we were in eleventh grade and another tragedy struck the O'Byrne family.

The photo was taken many years before, back when Bevy and I were still children, Benjamin was still alive, the happy, smiling adults in the photo knew nothing about grief and the island wasn't filled with talk of war. Staring up at me are both sets of parents, sitting around the dining room table at my parents' house playing Bridge with happy smiles on their faces. My father has his arm around my mother's shoulder and Mrs. O'Byrne is kissing Mr. O'Byrne on the cheek. The table in front of them is littered with playing cards and whiskey tumblers. I run my fingertips over the glass, trying to remember Bevy's parents like this. For so many years, I never even saw Mrs. O'Byrne, let alone remember her smiling. Mr. O'Byrne, who used to like to tease me and ruffle my hair, barely looked at me after Benjamin died and certainly never said another word to me, teasing or otherwise.

Dropping my hand from the photo, I head back over to the couch and ease my tired body slowly back down on the cushions. Picking up my pen and paper, I write about the day that made Bevy hate everything about this beautiful island we called home and the moment in time that started me on my path to falling in love with Beverly O'Byrne.

Fear makes you see things that you never even noticed, things that were right in front of you the whole time. The fear of losing Bevy changed everything for me.

Chapter 7

March 1951

A WADDED UP piece of paper smacks me square in the chest and I drop my pencil, shooting Bevy a dirty look across the kitchen table as she laughs. I just got home from work at the bank. As usual, I'd brought work home and I have a bunch of things to add to the ledgers before I can relax. Bevy is supposed to be studying for a test tomorrow, but she keeps interrupting me. Billy, who's sitting next to Bevy, wads up another piece of paper and throws it at me. Neither one of them can be serious for five minutes.

After Billy and I graduated last year, I went to work with my father at the bank straightaway and have been slowly dying inside since. Billy took a job working construction on the mainland and has been taking the ferry back and forth every day. The project he's working on now is a hotel in downtown Beaufort, and he comes home with his hands covered with dirt and grime and his shirt sweat-stained. Glancing down at my perfectly pressed dress shirt and my clean hands, I curse under my breath. I've never wanted to switch places with anyone more in my life than I do with Billy right now. He gets to be out in the sunshine all day long while I'm stuck in a cold, dark office, staring at numbers for so long that I'm pretty sure I'm going cross-eyed.

"I'm tired of studying for this stupid Geometry test. Let's go for a walk or something," Bevy complains, leaning back in the kitchen chair to stare out of the small window next to her. "We should go inside the lighthouse so I can practice my solo for this weekend. I love the echo in that place."

Billy and I share a look as Bevy turns to face us.

"What? What's wrong with that? Do you guys have a better idea?" she asks.

"Better than sitting there listening to you screech while my ears bleed?" Billy jokes.

Bevy wads up another piece of paper and throws this one right at Billy's face.

"I do NOT screech, you jerk!"

I laugh right along with Billy, even if Bevy *is* right. She definitely doesn't screech. Her voice is like an angel, and even though I'd never tell another soul, I get all warm inside when I see her close her eyes and sing. It's embarrassing and definitely not something I need anyone else knowing. Bevy is my friend. I don't understand the feelings that come over me when I hear her sing. It makes me feel like I need to hold her hand, wrap her up in my arms and all of the other things boyfriends do. She's only a junior in high school and from what I've heard, has plenty of boys chasing after her. As a grown man with a job and responsibilities, I have no business feeling like this for a high school girl, especially one who's my best friend.

"You know, speaking of your screeching," Billy says, laughing and shielding his face with his hands as Bevy readies another piece of paper to lob at him, "I saw a flier in town about an open mic night at a club on the mainland next weekend. It's at the Uptown Lounge and anyone can get up and sing. You have to be eighteen to get in, but a guy we went to school with works the door. I bet I could get him to let you in."

I watch as Bevy's face lights up and her eyes sparkle. I've heard of the Uptown Lounge. Loud music, lots of drinking and plenty of unsavory characters and goings-on, it's definitely not a place for the likes of my sweet, innocent Bevy. I can just picture her standing up on stage, looking all pretty and singing her heart out while drunken men in the audience yell crude things to her. There's no way I'm going to let that happen.

"You're not singing at the Uptown Lounge," I tell her, picking up my pencil and going back to my work.

Bevy leans forward and rests her arms on the table. "What do you mean, I'm *not* singing at the Uptown Lounge? You can't tell me what to do, Trip Fisher. I'm seventeen years old and if I want to sing at a lounge, I'm going to sing at a lounge. You heard Billy, he knows someone who can get us in. Right, Billy?"

I give Billy a look that clearly says *shut your mouth and don't encourage her*, but he ignores me.

"Yep, John Gates. You remember him, don't you, Trip? He was on our basketball team in the ninth grade."

I shake my head and sigh. "Oh, you mean the John Gates who dropped out of school in tenth grade to rob liquor stores and race dragsters? Yes, he sounds like the exact person I want doing Bevy a favor."

I glance over at Bevy and she's still glaring at me. The sun is shining brightly through the window next to her, making her look even more like an angel than ever before. She did something different to her hair today. Instead of her usual ponytail, her hair is hanging long and curly all around her face. She looks…pretty. I've always thought Bevy had a nice face, but there's just something about her today and I can't stop staring. She purses her lips and I wonder what it would be like to kiss her, causing a fluttering feeling in my stomach that is almost instantly replaced by horror. I've got no business thinking about my *friend* this way when I've been dating Kathy Sanders. Kathy moved to the island a few months ago and we've been to the movies and to dinner every weekend since the day she came into the bank with her mother. Why am I thinking about kissing Bevy when I've got a perfectly nice, beautiful girlfriend? Stupid Bevy and her stupid, pretty face.

"You don't want to go to that club, Bevy. It's dirty and it's not the type of place you want to sing. Finish studying so I can get this work done and then we can do something fun."

She sighs and everything goes back to

normal. I try to concentrate on the ledger instead of Bevy's fresh, floral scent. I think about checks and balances and refuse to stare as Bevy tucks a loose strand of hair behind her ear, wondering if her hair is soft and smooth now that it's not pulled back into a tight ponytail.

I listen to Billy mutter under his breath about how stupid Geometry is and how Bevy will never use it when she's older, so there's no point in studying. Bevy crosses her legs under the table, one of them sliding gently against mine. I start to break out in a cold sweat and my pencil falls from my hand and clatters to the table. Bevy looks up at me in confusion right when the telephone rings in the living room.

Bevy opens her mouth, most likely to ask me why I'm staring at her like a fool, when we hear my mother shout in agony from the other room. All three of us jump up from the table and race to the living room, finding her crumpled on the floor next to the end table, sobbing. I've never seen my mother break down like this and my feet feel like they're glued to the floor. Bevy rushes over to her, bends down and wraps her arms around my mother's shoulders. I watch as my mother

WORTH THE TRIP

turns and holds Bevy's face in her hands while the tears stream down her cheeks.

"Bevy, oh, my sweet Bevy," my mother whispers through her tears. "I'm so sorry, honey. I'm so sorry. Your mother…it's your mother."

Bevy shakes her head back and forth in denial while Billy and I continue to stand in the doorway, watching the scene unfold in front of us like spectators at a baseball game.

Bevy has always clung to the hope that one day her mother would snap out of her depression, that she'd eventually pull up the shades, let the sunlight in and begin living again. Based on my mother's announcement, I have a feeling that's never going to happen.

"She's gone, Bevy. I'm so sorry," my mother tells her softly.

"How? I…HOW? I just saw her this morning before school and she was fine," Bevy whispers in confusion. "I mean, she was in bed, like always, but she actually smiled at me when I went in to tell her good-bye before I left. She was fine. I just saw her and she was FINE!"

Her voice gets louder and my mother closes her eyes for a few moments before opening them back up to stare sadly at Bevy.

47

"She took her own life, honey."

At my mother's words, I watch Bevy's shoulders fall and it's almost like watching the life drain right out of her. She quickly stands up and backs away. My mother quickly gets up and reaches for her, but Bevy shrugs out of her reach.

I take a step in Bevy's direction, but I have no idea what to do. I didn't know how to help her when I was nine and her brother was killed, and I'm even more clueless at nineteen now that her mother is gone.

Without a word, Bevy turns and runs past me, the front door slamming closed behind her.

"Go on, you go after Bevy and I'll call your dad," Billy tells me as I look back and forth between the front door and my mother.

"It's okay, Trip. Go to Bevy, she needs you. I'll be fine," my mother says as she wipes the tears from her cheeks.

Even though Mrs. O'Byrne's depression tore their friendship apart, my mother never stopped trying. She still went to Bevy's house several times a week in an attempt to bring her friend back to her. Part of me wants to stay with my mother, but I know I can't help her. I don't know if I can help Bevy, either, but I need to try.

Giving my mom a quick hug, I take off, instinctively heading towards the lighthouse. I immediately see Bevy's footprints in the sand and I'm thankful that I know her so well. A few minutes later, I find her sitting at the base of the lighthouse with her legs pulled up to her chest and her head buried in her knees. I walk up to her slowly so I don't scare her and take a seat on the sand next to her.

Listening to her soft, muffled cries, I want to scream and throw something. I can't stand Bevy hurting like this. I want to go back to twenty minutes ago, when she was throwing paper and irritated with me.

"I'm sorry, Bevy. I'm so sorry," I tell her, not sure of what else to say.

"I HATE this place. I hate this damn island!" she suddenly shouts, pushing up from the sand and stalking towards the water's edge.

I scramble up and follow her, shocked at her anger and hearing her curse.

She picks up a large rock from the sand and throws it as hard as she can into the water, screaming at the top of her lungs.

"I HATE THIS PLACE! I WANT TO LEAVE AND NEVER COME BACK!"

My mouth drops open in shock as Bevy continues picking up rocks and throwing them angrily into the waves.

"You don't mean that," I mutter as she continues to shout her hatred about the beautiful place we live.

She whirls around angrily and glares at me. "Of course I mean it! Everywhere I look, this stupid place is filled with sadness. I've had to walk around this island with Benjamin's ghost on my heels for years, and now I'll have to do the same thing with my mother. I hate it here. I hate it here so much! Why wasn't I enough for her? What is so wrong with me that she couldn't love me enough and STAY?!"

Her anger immediately dies and she crumbles right in front of me. I fly forward and catch her in my arms before she hits the sand, pulling her close and wrapping my arms around her while she sobs into my shoulder.

I hug her tightly to me and rock us gently back and forth, trying to soothe her cries.

She feels so good in my arms that for a second, I almost forget her mother just died and she wants to leave the island, that she wants to leave ME behind. Her floral scent wraps around me and she slides her arms around my waist, making my heart skip a beat. I run my hand down the back of her head, finding her hair just as soft as I thought it would be.

"You are MORE than enough, Bevy. You are beautiful and smart, funny and courageous. Don't you ever think for one second that there is anything wrong with you," I tell her as I hug her even tighter. "You are loved, Bevy. You are loved so much."

She cries harder and I tell her I'll do anything to make it better. I promise her we can go anywhere and do anything she wants. I tell her that no matter what, I will always be here for her. I will never leave her like her brother and her mother and I mean it with everything inside of me. Wherever Beverly O'Byrne goes, I will follow.

I feel my heart beating in tune with Bevy's as our chests press tightly together and we continue holding onto each other as the sun sets over the horizon and her tears finally subside.

I refuse to let go of her, even though she's not crying anymore, and I think about a line in a movie Bevy dragged me to a few months ago. Something about how your heart beats for another person. I remember Bevy punching me in the arm and shushing me as I laughed over the actor's words, but in this moment, they make perfect sense and I absolutely understand the sentiment. I feel like my heart is only beating now because of the girl in my arms and I wonder if this is what love feels like.

Chapter 8

MRS. O'BYRNE WOKE up on March 19, 1951 and decided she could no longer take the grief of living without her son. After ten long years, she'd had enough. When Mr. O'Byrne left for work and Bevy headed to school, she loaded Mr. O'Byrne's Smith and Wesson .38 Special, put it in her mouth and pulled the trigger.

Bevy, true to her word, wanted away from Fisher's Island and would have done anything to make it happen, including sneaking out of her bedroom window one Friday night, taking the ferry to the mainland and singing at the Uptown Lounge. She knew how I felt about that place and her singing there and thought it best not to include me in her plans. Since Billy was in on her little adventure and even accompanied her so she wouldn't be alone, I refused to speak to either one of them for weeks after I found out. I tried to tell myself that I was only angry because Bevy could have been hurt in that seedy joint, but to be honest, I was jealous. Jealous because, for the first time in our lives, she'd kept something from me. She didn't trust me with her secret and it killed me. I turned into such an asshole, I'm surprised Bevy never punched me in the face.

I wasn't able to ignore my best friend for long, but that didn't mean things between us weren't completely different. For the next year, the teasing of our younger years was back in full force. I picked on her whenever I could, and looking back now, I did a lot of things with the intention of making HER jealous. Of course, it all came back to bite me in the ass in the end. I was angry at Bevy for her constant chatter about how she couldn't wait to leave the island and I was angry that my feelings for her were changing and she didn't even seem to notice. Every day I spent with her for the next year, I made fun of stupid, little things, when all I really wanted to do was tell her that I thought I was falling in love with her.

"Your hair looks really dumb like that."
It's shiny and beautiful and I want to run my fingers through it.

"You're wearing THAT just to go for a walk? You look ridiculous."
You should wear blue dresses all the time be-

cause they make your eyes sparkle and you look beautiful in them.

"Uuugggh, fine, take my hand. I guess I can help you up the rocks."

Hold my hand forever and never let go.

Flipping to the next page in the album, I smile down at the picture of Bevy looking more beautiful than I had ever seen her. She's smiling brightly at the camera and I look like a schmuck as I stare at *her*. It really is a great picture, but I remember hating my mother when she had it developed and couldn't stop laughing. She handed it to me and said "This, right here, is where I think you finally saw what has been right in front of you this entire time."

Little did my mother know, I'd seen it a while ago, but that moment is where it finally occurred to me just what I was looking at – my future.

Chapter 9

May 1952

LEANING AGAINST MY car with my arms crossed, I try not to make it too obvious that I've been staring at Bevy since she walked out of school and started talking with a group of her friends a few feet away. I give her a ride home from school whenever I get out of the bank early and the best part of my day is standing here in front of the school and watching her before she sees me. I can't help but be mesmerized by Bevy with her head thrown back in laughter, as if she doesn't have a care in the world.

Her pretty hair is pulled up into a ponytail and I watch as she tucks a stray piece of her long bangs behind one ear, an unconscious move that I've seen her do a thousand times over the years, but one I've secretly become enamored with lately. The sound of her laughter surrounds me and Billy smacks me on the back before she notices that I'm staring at her like a lovesick fool.

"Did you pick me up from the ferry just so I could watch you moon all over Bevy?"

I clear my throat and look away from her, studying a very interesting rock down by my feet.

"Shut up or I'll make you walk home," I warn him.

It's Bevy's senior year of high school, and there's only a handful of weeks left until graduation and one week until her senior prom. Every day I pick her up from school, I hold my breath and wait to hear her tell me that some jerk has asked her to the dance. As much as I want to ask Bevy to go with *me*, it just wouldn't be right. I graduated two years ago. How silly would I look going to a high school dance? Age difference notwithstanding, I've been a complete jerk to her lately and she'd probably laugh in my face. Instead of telling her how I feel, I've done the exact opposite and made it seem like I don't care about her at all.

I want to laugh at myself for even entertaining the idea of asking her to prom. I've been dating Kathy off and on for a year now, but I'd never asked her to go steady and I heard she went on a date with someone else last week. It must not have gone well, because she was certainly hinting around my asking her back out when I ran into her in town yesterday. I like Kathy well enough, she's a nice girl and okay to hang out with, but I can't see myself spending the rest of my life with her. There's only one girl I could imagine playing that big of a role in my future and she's standing a few feet away. That thought has grown so big over the last year, I'm surprised I'm able to think about anything else.

Since Mrs. O'Bryne's death, Bevy has been focused on singing and consumed by thoughts of becoming a big star. It's all she ever talks about, and I know if I don't make my move soon, she's really going to leave and I might never see her again. With graduation so close, it's only a matter of time before she takes off. I can't let her do that without letting her know how I feel.

"Will you just quit being an idiot and ask her out already?" Billy says loudly, making me jump and stare at him in shock.

"What? What are you talking about? Ask who what?" I reply, pulling my car keys out of my pocket and fiddling with them.

"Oh, give it a rest, Trip!" Billy says with a laugh. "You might be able to hide it from *her,* but you can't hide it from me. I see the way you're always staring at Bevy, smiling like an idiot when she says something nice to you and going out of your way to pretend like you don't care."

I try not to blush and roll my eyes at him instead. "I have no idea what you're talking about."

Billy continues laughing and shakes his head at me.

"If you say one word to her, I'll never speak to you again," I threaten.

Billy holds his hands up in surrender. "Jeez, I promise, I promise. "Prom is only a week away. If you want to take Bevy, you better hurry up and ask before some other guy beats you to it and steals her away."

"Bevy isn't going to go to the dance," I scoff, trying really hard to make myself believe what I'm saying. "She hates dances and besides, no one has asked her yet."

"I heard Bob Miller is going to ask her."

My eyes widen and my mouth drops open in shock. Bob Miller is a jerk. He was a jerk when Billy and I were in school and word around town is that he's gotten worse. He goes out with a new girl every week and there's talk that he likes to take them parking in his car. As soon as he gets some time alone with them, he dumps them and moves on to the next girl. I'm not going to allow *my* Bevy to become one of his "girls."

Just then, Bevy says goodbye to her friends and bounces over to us, her long hair swishing back and forth behind her head as she stops in front of me.

"I hate Mrs. Goran. I swear she calls on me every time I don't know an answer. It's like she's a mind reader and does it on purpose. If I don't study for the Chemistry test tomorrow, I'm going to be in big trouble," she rambles as I stare over her shoulder and see Bob Miller headed this way.

Bevy waves her hand in front of my face to get my attention. "Hello? Earth to Trip."

Bob is walking faster and my stomach suddenly plummets to my feet. It's now or never.

"Listen, Bevy, I think…maybe we should…you know next week….I was just thinking…"

Billy snickers next to me and I punch him in the arm without taking my eyes off of Bevy. She's patiently waiting for me to stop stuttering and make some actual sense, but I can't get the words out.

"Yes?" she asks softly, taking a step towards me.

She's so pretty that my mind goes blank. This is Bevy. MY Bevy. Why is it so hard to just ask her? Ask her if she wants to go on a date. Shit, just ask her to prom! Who cares if I'm twenty years old and going back to high school, at least I'll be with Bevy. Just say it already!

"Hey, Beverly! Do you have a second?"

Bob comes up next to us and Bevy slowly looks away from me. I want to grab onto her face and pull her gaze back to mine. Why is she looking at stupid Bob Miller?

"Oh, hey, Bob," Bevy greets him with a smile.

I want to punch my fist into the passenger window of my car when she smiles at him. She shouldn't be allowed to smile at anyone but me. I feel like a giant child, but I can't help it.

"How about you go with me to the prom next week?" Bob asks her casually, leaning his shoulder against the side of MY car and sliding his hands into the front pocket of his jeans.

Not only do I want to punch the window, I want to punch that smug smirk right off of Bob's face. He's standing there thinking Bevy is going to jump at the chance to go anywhere with him.

Bevy looks back over her shoulder at me expectantly, like she's waiting for me to say something. What the hell am I supposed to say? Don't go with Bob Miller because he's a jerk? You should go with me because I'm in love with you?

Instead, I chicken out and pick option three, giving her a shrug because I honestly think she's going to laugh in Bob's face. I watch as Bevy's face falls and she turns back to look at Bob, giving him a shrug of her own.

"Um, sure, I guess. That would be nice," Bevy tells him.

"Yikes," Billy mumbles next to me.

I listen to Bob and Bevy make plans, staring with my mouth wide open at the exchange going on right in front of me, suddenly feeling like the ham sandwich I had for lunch is going to come up all over my shoes.

When Bob finally walks away, giving me a wave and telling me we should catch up sometime, I shoot him a dirty look and don't say a word. I can't believe this just happened.

After Bob disappears into the crowd of students in the parking lot, Bevy turns towards me and I'm surprised I don't see a huge smile on her face after landing a date to prom with the most popular guy in school.

"You are NOT going to the dance with Bob Miller!" I tell her.

Bevy puts her hands on her hips and glares at me.

"You can't tell me what to do! Bob is a very nice guy and at least he asked!"

It's almost like she wanted me to be the one who asked her, but that's impossible. I'd know if Bevy wanted me to ask her, I'm sure of it.

I move closer to her, mirroring her pose with my own hands on my hips. "Bob is NOT a nice guy and I don't want you going to the dance with him."

I can practically see the smoke coming out of Bevy's ears.

"You can't tell me what to do, Trip Fisher!" she shouts.

"I most certainly CAN!"

She stomps her foot and crosses her arms in front of her. "I'm going to the prom with Bob, so stow it!"

Bevy has never liked Kathy, always calling her a snob and saying that she only cares about looking pretty all time so she can catch a rich husband and spend all his money. I'm so angry at the thought of Bevy going to prom with Bob that the next words fly out of my mouth without a second thought.

"FINE! Then I'm going to have Kathy come over and keep me company while you're busy on your *little date*!"

Bevy rolls her eyes. "I can't believe you're going to ask her out again when you know very well she only likes you because your dad owns the bank."

Billy laughs and I feel my face redden because Bevy doesn't know how to speak quietly. There's also the fact that she's kind of right. Kathy's always asking why my family doesn't buy a bigger home since we have so much money and she works so hard at buttering up my parents that it's almost sickening. I want to tell Bevy that Kathy doesn't hold a candle her, but I stick my foot a little deeper in my mouth instead.

"Now we both have dates. Maybe we should double. Oooh, I have a better idea. Kathy and I can be chaperones! I'll just go inside and ask the principal if he needs more volunteers."

What the hell am I saying? This is a horrible idea!

Billy laughs, but I ignore him.

"Oh, that sounds like a fine idea," Bevy tells me sweetly. A little *too* sweetly. "I'll have Bob pick me up at your house, since I'm sure your mom is going to want to help me get ready, and then we can all go together."

I really expected her to protest the idea of a double date, not go along with it. My anger and jealousy boils hotter thinking about Bob sliding a corsage on Bevy's wrist, Bob holding her hand, Bob putting his hands on her while they dance.

"Since when do you want to go to the dance, anyway? You don't even like dances! You know you have to get dressed up and actually look nice for a change, right? You have to brush your hair and keep your dress clean!"

Billy whistles under his breath and takes a step back from us as Bevy drops her hands to her sides and clenches her hands into fists.

"YOU are a JERK, Trip Fisher! I'm not going home with you, I'd rather walk," Bevy whispers before she turns and runs away.

If she had screamed those words at me, I would have fired something equally insulting right back, but seeing the tears pool in her eyes and hearing the hurt in her voice stops me from shouting at her as she disappears around the corner of the school.

"I can't believe she's going to the dance with Bob Miller!" I shout, kicking my foot angrily against the tire of my car.

"I can't believe you're such an idiot," Billy tells me with a sad shake of his head.

BEVY HASN'T SPOKEN to me in a week, no matter how hard I've tried. I've thrown so many rocks at her bedroom window that I'm surprised the glass hasn't gotten weak and shattered.

She came over an hour ago so my mom could help her get ready. When I opened the door, she shouldered right past me and up the stairs without a word. I wish she would let me apologize so we could get past this. I hate having Bevy mad at me.

I've been shooting Bob dirty looks ever since he got here and feel like an idiot when he asks me where Kathy is. Obviously, Bevy enlightened him of my genius plan of serving as chaperone. Instead of telling him the truth, that I never even called Kathy because I don't want anything to do with her, I lie and tell him she had other plans. While Bob goes on and on about how he beat the free-throw record I set my senior year, I tune him out.

I want to tell Bevy I'm sorry for being such a jerk, but she's been closed upstairs with my mother in her bedroom and neither one of them answered when I knocked.

A few minutes later, I hear the stairs creak and Bob whistles under his breath. I turn my head and my mouth drops open in shock.

Bevy is slowly making her way down the stairs, holding onto the railing with one hand and bunching up some of the fabric of her long skirt in the other so she doesn't trip. At least I *think* it's Bevy. I've never seen her look like this before. She looks gorgeous. I mean, Bevy has always been a pretty girl, she's just never done anything special to make herself *more* pretty like a lot of girls. It's never mattered much to me because when I look at her, she always looks like the most beautiful girl in the world, but right now, I am amazed. Tonight, she's wearing a pale blue dress that hangs off of her shoulders and her hair is piled up on top of her head. She has on just a tiny hint of makeup and, next to her dress, her eyes look like big, blue swimming pools.

When she gets to the bottom of the stairs, she walks across the room and right past me to Bob. He tells her how pretty she looks and slides the corsage he brought onto her wrist. I want to rip it off and throw it across the room, to tell him to keep his hands off of her because she's MY Bevy, not his. I want to ask her why she got all gussied up for BOB MIL-LER and not me.

My mom takes a few pictures of Bevy and Bob alone and then makes me get in one final picture as she gets her camera ready, telling us to smile. I can't smile and I can't stop staring at Bevy. I hear the flash of the camera and don't even care that I wasn't looking at my mom when she took it.

My mom tells them to have a great time and stands in the open doorway, waving as they disappear from sight. I stomp upstairs to my room, slamming my door so hard I'm surprised it doesn't break.

A few hours later, lying on my back, staring up at my ceiling and trying not to think about what Bevy and Bob are doing, I hear something smack against my window. I quickly get up, throw my window open and see Bevy standing down in the grass with her shoes in her hand and a smile on her face as she looks up at me.

"Get down here and walk me home like a gentleman!" she shouts.

"I thought you already had a gentleman to do that for you?" I yell back, trying not to sound like a jealous jerk, wondering if Bob held her too close, if he tried to kiss her, and if she wants me to walk her home just so she can gush about all of those things.

"You were right, he's a jerk. He danced with another girl most of the night and then left early with her. So, are you going to walk me home or not?"

I try not to smile, realizing Bevy didn't have as great a time at the dance as I imagined. Racing down the stairs, I meet her outside and we walk side-by-side through town towards her house. We usually have lots of things to talk about, but tonight, it feels like the weight of the world is on my shoulders and I'm having a hard time telling her what I want to say.

"What's wrong, Trip?" Bevy asks me softly as we get to her driveway.

I want to tell her that everything is wrong. Bevy should have been MY date tonight, not Bob's. I would have held her close and danced with her all night, I would have made her happy and I never would have left her side. I'm afraid of what I feel for her. Everything is changing and it scares me. I don't want to lose her as a friend, but I need more than just her friendship. I need her to tell me that she'd never really leave the island because she couldn't stand the thought of being apart from me. I need her to love me as much as I love her, but what if she doesn't? What will happen to us if I blurt out my feelings and she doesn't share them? I can't take that chance. Even if I have to love Bevy from afar for the rest of my life, at least she'll still BE in my life. If I screw up our friendship, she may never speak to me again.

"Nothing is wrong, Bevy. I'm just sorry you didn't have a good time tonight," I tell her instead, forcing a smile on my face.

"So, why didn't Kathy come tonight? I thought you were going to be chaperones?" she asks me with a smirk, knowing full well that I only threw that Kathy nonsense at her to tick her off.

I shrug and slide my hands into my pockets as we walk up her front porch stairs. "You were right about her. She only cares about how much money I make."

WORTH THE TRIP

We share a laugh as I open the screen door and she steps inside.

"Thanks for walking me home, Trip," Bevy says with a smile as she starts to back away from me into the house. I want to stay, I want to pull her into my arms and tell her I'm in love with her. I want to say so many things, but nothing comes out as I watch her move further away from me.

I let go of the screen door and it starts to slam shut when Bevy quickly pushes it back open. She comes out on the porch and stands right in front of me.

I hold my breath, wondering if maybe she really does feel something for me and she's going to be the one to say it first. Bevy does like to win at everything.

That thought puts a smile on my face until Bevy opens her mouth and speaks in a rush.

"So, remember when I sang at the Uptown Lounge last year? Well, I guess there was record producer in the audience that night, and he started asking around about me. John Gates gave him my phone number. Anyway, this guy is a big time producer in California and he wants me to come out there and sing on a record. A real, live record! I leave the day before graduation."

My mouth opens and closes like a fish out of water.

"You're honestly going to leave before graduation?" I ask dumbly.

She shrugs. "Who cares about graduation? I could be a huge star, Trip! All of my dreams are coming true. I don't care about a stupid diploma. I already finished finals and I know I passed. It's not like I'll be missing much if I don't go."

Me. You'll be missing me. Please, tell me that you'll miss me.

Everything I know I should say to her is right there, on the tip of my tongue, but I don't say anything at all as she disappears inside.

I wish I had told her that she's the most beautiful girl I've ever seen. I wish I had told her that I love her and that *I* could make all of her dreams come true. I wish I hadn't wasted so much time being an idiot.

Chapter 10

I RUN MY fingers over the prom night photo and curse myself a hundred times. Closing my eyes for a few minutes, I try to will away all of the aches and pains in my tired, old body. I don't have time to be sick or to worry about my health. I have to get these words on paper before it's too late. Picking the notepad and pen back up, I continue writing my and Bevy's story.

If ever a boy needed a good, solid whack upside the head, it was me. I spent the next few weeks after prom being a complete dumbass where Bevy was concerned. Keenly aware of the clock ticking down on our time together, I spent every free moment at Bevy's side, forgoing sleep altogether in exchange for throwing rocks at her bedroom window and sneaking down to the lighthouse. Sitting together under the stars, we talked about everything, including how much I hated working at the bank. She was going to make something of herself and I was going to be stuck working for Fisher's Bank and Trust for the rest of my life.

Being cooped up behind a desk was sucking out my very soul and I spent the days counting down the minutes until I could run out that stuffy building, tear off my suit and tie and get into the sunshine. I'd spent my off time the last few years helping people fix things around the island, a side job that had grown out of serving as Billy's assistant on a few remodeling projects. A couple of local contractors had taken notice and taken me under their wings, showing me how to use a hammer and fix a leaky pipe. When I got off work at the bank, I yanked my suit off as fast as I could, threw on an old t-shirt and a pair of jeans and ran back into town to get another lesson on fix-it work. Regardless of how much money I stood to make at the bank, there was nothing I'd rather spend my days doing than working with my hands. In typical Bevy fashion, she told me to stop being a chicken and tell my father how I felt, that there was no point living your life doing something that made you unhappy.

I laid my heart bare to Beverly O'Bryne over the course of those weeks, discussing everything except, of course, the only think that really mattered. I noticed things about

Bevy I'd never taken the time to see and imagined how I would feel when she was gone, nearly making myself physically ill. I noticed how her laugh made my heart beat fast and how her smile, especially when it was aimed at me, made me feel like I hung the moon. All I could think about was Bevy leaving our island and how I might never see her again. So much wasted time. If only I'd have pulled my head out of my ass sooner.

With the photo album resting next to me on the couch, I flip the page and stare down at a picture of Bevy in her cap and gown. Bevy had no plans of walking with her class-mates at graduation, but I was the only one who knew that—or so I thought. When she brought home her packaged cap and gown from school that day, Bevy tried it on and asked my mom to take a picture. Right before my mom snapped it, Bevy whispered in my ear, "This will be a nice photo to have, since I won't actually be at graduation."

In the photo, Bevy has a huge smile on her face and I look like someone ran over my favorite dog. My arm is around her shoulder and she's got hers wrapped around my waist. She's smiling so bright at the camera because her whole life was just beginning. She had a plan that night and was so excited she could have burst. All I could think about in that moment was facing forever without her. I didn't want her to go, but I had no idea how to make her stay. Flipping to the next page in the notepad, I shake out the tingling in my hand and continue writing.

Chapter 11

June 1952

SHE'S LEAVING.

The nightmare that's plagued me from the moment she screamed how much she hated this island is coming true. Bevy is packing up and leaving me behind. When I stopped by her house earlier, she snuck me up to her bedroom (not that her father would have even noticed), showing me her packed suitcases as she explained her plan to leave on the last ferry off the island tonight. I told her she was crazy and asked if she really thought she was good enough to become a singing star and we got into a huge fight. I never should have said those things. I'd lashed out in desperation and anger, intentionally hurting her, something I hated myself for.

She was supposed to come over for dinner tonight to celebrate her last day of school with us and my father has been asking where she is for the last hour. I didn't have the heart to tell him that our Bevy is leaving us, that we might never see her again. I couldn't bring myself to say the words out loud.

I'm angry that she can just pack up and leave me without giving it a second thought and I'm jealous that she can so easily follow her dreams when I can't even tell my own father that I want nothing to do with Fisher's Bank and Trust. I'm miserable every day I spend inside that building. I like working with my hands, I like fixing things and getting dirty. I don't want to wear a suit and be stuck inside for the rest of my life. I want to tell my father that I can't follow in his footsteps, but I just don't have the guts to do it. I'm not like Bevy. My father has groomed me to take over the bank since it opened. How can I just break his heart and tell him it's not what I want? How can Bevy just break my heart and leave me? Why does all of this have to be so hard?

As I pace back and forth in the hallway by the front door, my mother walks quietly up behind me and puts a hand on my shoulder. I stop pacing and turn to face her. She smiles softly and pulls me in for a hug.

"I love you, son. I love the man that you've become and I'm so proud of you."

I swallow back tears and hug her back,

not feeling much like a man in this moment. Tomorrow, Bevy will no longer be here to laugh at my jokes and challenge me to be a better person. For the first time in my life, I don't want tomorrow to come.

My mom pulls away and presses her hands to either side of my face. "No matter what choices you make in life, your father and I will still love you. But I'm telling you right now, if you don't go after that girl, you're going to regret it the rest of your life."

I look at her in confusion, wondering how she could possibly know what's going on in my head. "I'm not a stupid woman, my boy. I know what Bevy is planning on doing tonight. We've talked about it a few times and she asked for my advice."

"Let me guess, you told her to go?" I ask angrily.

"Why should she stay, Trip? Yes, I'm worried about her, but you and I both know her father is never going to love that girl like she deserves and give her the attention she needs. Now that her mother is gone, I told her to follow her dreams, something that girl should've done a long time ago. I'm telling you the exact same thing right now. I know you don't want to work at the bank and your father knows it, as well. He's just too stubborn to say anything. I also know you've been in love with Bevy longer than you care to admit. If you want something badly enough, you can't be afraid to go after it. If you want to be a handyman on the island, do it. If you want to be with Bevy, *do it*. There's nothing stopping you but your own fears."

I look away from my mother and take a deep breath. Bevy has been through a lot on this island. I know she wants to get away from the memories, but I need her here with me. I need to prove to her that I can erase all of the bad things and fill them with good.

"What if she turns me down?"

She pulls my face back towards her and stares deeply into my eyes. "You'll never know unless you try."

Her hands drop from my cheeks and she leans up and kisses both of them before giving me a smile and heading back towards the kitchen to finish dinner.

"The ferry leaves in twenty minutes," she yells over her shoulder before disappearing around the corner.

I don't even hesitate before racing out the front door and down the steps of the porch to my car. I peel out of the driveway and make it to the ferry on the other end of the island just as the sun begins to set over the water. Jumping out of the car, I jog along the dock filled with people heading back to the mainland, my eyes peeled for brown curly hair and bright blue eyes in the sea of faces.

I spot her standing by the roped off area next to the moveable walkway that will be hooked up to the ferry as soon as it docks. She's got a suitcase clutched in both of her hands and one at her feet. I take a few moments to stare at her from a distance as she watches the boat slowly make its way towards the dock. She's so beautiful it takes my breath away. She's been my whole world for as long as I can remember and I can't imagine spending even one day without her here to share my life. I shouldn't have waited so long to tell her how I feel and I'm scared to death I might be too late.

Pushing my way through the crowd of people, I stop right next to Bevy, lean down and pick up the suitcase from the ground. She turns and looks at me in surprise, gasping when I snatch the second suitcase out of her hands. Without saying a word, I turn and walk away from her, weaving in and out of the crowd of people waiting for the ferry as fast as I can.

"TRIP! What are you doing? Will you get back here, the boat is almost here!" she shouts after me.

I pick up my pace until I'm jogging down the dock and I hear her footsteps pounding behind me.

"PUT DOWN MY SUITCASES RIGHT NOW, TRIP FISHER!" she yells as I jump off the dock and onto the sand.

I move down the beach hurriedly until I feel her hand wrap around my arm and yank me to a stop. Tossing her suitcases to the sand, I turn around to face her. She's got her hands on her hips and she's really angry.

"Trip! What has gotten into you? Give me my suitcases!" she demands.

She leans down to pick them up and I block her way. When she stomps her foot, I can't help but laugh.

"Do you think this is *funny*? The ferry is going to leave without me, Trip. This is NOT funny!" she shouts.

She moves towards her suitcases again and I put my hands on her upper arms, stopping her.

"Don't leave."

Bevy stares at me like I've lost my mind

WORTH THE TRIP

and I can't blame her.

"What are you talking about? I have to leave. I have a meeting with the record producer tomorrow," she reminds me.

"Don't leave," I beg again, moving closer to her.

"Give me one good reason why I shouldn't leave?" she challenges, lifting her chin and glaring at me.

"Because you just can't leave. You need to stay here, with me."

She huffs and pulls out of my arms, shaking her head at me before turning and heading back towards the ferry.

"Not good enough. Forget the suitcases, I don't need them. I'll just buy new clothes with all of the money I'm going to make when I sing on my first record!"

She's walking away from me and I start to panic. This is not how this was supposed to go. I'm messing everything up and she's still going to leave me.

"I LOVE YOU, BEVY! PLEASE, DON'T LEAVE!" I shout after her.

She stops in her tracks, but doesn't turn to face me. I jog over to her and stand right behind her, wanting more than anything to put my arms around her, so I do. Wrapping my arms around her waist, I pull her body back against mine. I rest my chin on her shoulder and put my lips close to her ear, telling her everything I should have told her a long time ago.

"You can't leave because I'm in love with you, Bevy. I've probably been in love with you since the first time you threw sand at me, and I am a fool for not telling you before now. I love you. I love everything about you. I love that you challenge me and I love that you can run faster than me. I love that I can tell you anything and you won't judge me. I love that you're my best friend and I love that you make me laugh. I love you, Beverly O'Byrne, and I don't want to spend even one day without you. I know this island is filled with sadness and bad memories for you, but if you give me a chance, just give me one chance, I will erase all of those bad memories and replace them with good ones."

She turns in my arms and I see tears falling down her face. I'm not sure whether they're happy tears or sad tears, but I don't allow myself time to second guess what I've done. Instead, I follow my dreams, exactly like my mother told me I should do. Grabbing both of her hands, I drop down on one knee on the sand at her feet and stare up at her beautiful, tear-stained face.

"I'm sorry, I love you, please forgive me. I should've told you this sooner. I never should've wasted one minute of my time with you. Marry me, Bevy. Stay here and marry me. Please, don't leave me," I beg.

The loud horn of the ferry echoes in the distance and Bevy closes her eyes. I'm scared to death she's going to say no. My hands are sweating as I clutch tightly to hers and pray to God that I'm not too late.

Bevy finally opens her eyes, smiles down at me and sniffles.

"It's about damn time, Trip Fisher. I love you, I won't leave you, and of course I'll marry you."

My mouth drops open in shock and she laughs at me. The sound fills my heart with so much joy that it feels like it might burst right out of my chest. I jump up from the sand, pull her into my arms and lift her off of her feet. She wraps her arms around my shoulders and I swing her around in the sand as we both laugh. I finally stop twirling and set her down on her feet. She stares up into my eyes and tilts her head to the side.

"Say it again," she whispers.

I smile down at her and move my face closer to hers. "I love you."

Leaning even closer, I do something I've been dreaming about for longer than I can remember. I press my lips to hers and I kiss my Bevy for the first time. She kisses me back and it's like the whole world stops. The ocean waves crash against the shore at our feet and she sighs against my lips before she pulls away.

"I love you more," she tells me softly.

"Just remember who said it first," I tell her with a smile. Everything we do together seems to be a competition and it makes me feel good that for once in our life together, I beat her to the finish line.

She smacks me lightly on the chest with a laugh, bringing her lips back to mine.

Chapter 12

BEVY AND I grabbed her suitcases and ran as fast as we could to jump on the ferry before it left, laughing the entire way. We took that last ferry off of the island back to the mainland, applied for a marriage license and got married by a justice of the peace in the city before the ink was even dry. We celebrated our honeymoon with a single night at the Beaufort Inn, and it was the most wonderful night of my life up to that point. My parents were a little upset about us getting married without telling them, but we made it up to them by letting them throw us a huge wedding reception the following weekend. The entire island crowded into my parents' home to wish us well, with the notable exception of Mr. O'Byrne, who was just "too busy" to make it. Bevy brushed it off with a shrug, but I hugged her tighter than ever and promised her once again that I would replace all the bad memories with good ones. Bevy pushed aside her disappointment and convinced me to finally tell my father I couldn't work at the bank anymore once our guests departed. As my mother predicted, he smiled and told me he didn't care what I did, as long as I was happy.

I flip through the next few pages in the album, swiping angrily at the tears as they fall down my face. So many years of being happy and building a life together on this island. Pictures of our wedding reception, pictures of our first home, pictures of family picnics and holidays, pictures of me working out in the sunshine with a huge smile on my face…so many years and so many memories, but it wasn't long enough. It was never long enough.

The sun has come up and I take a few minutes to stare at the empty chair in the corner of the room. Upholstered in a heavy, red fabric, it was Bevy's favorite chair and it's never moved from that spot right next to the window. I can still see her sitting in that chair with her legs curled underneath her, writing in her journal. That woman loved to write things down. Every morning, she'd sit in that chair with a cup of coffee and write about her life. I always teased her about the horrible things she wrote about me, since she never allowed me to read the journals. She kept them in a shoebox in the back of our closet, and to this day, I have never touched them. They were her private thoughts, her dreams, her memories and I had no right to snoop through them, even though I wanted to. I wanted to know if she ever regretted staying on this island. If she ever looked back on the night I proposed and wished she had gotten on that ferry without me instead. No matter what I said to her in anger and fear, she really could have been a huge star. She could have lived the high life, never worrying whether there was enough money in the bank to buy groceries or to pay the mortgage. Whenever my insecurities got the best of me and I'd ask her if she had any regrets about not following her dreams and being stuck here with me, she would just shake her head and say "You silly man, how could I regret anything when I'm already living my dream?"

She told me writing things down helped her focus on the blessings in our life instead of the bad things, but I often wonder if she said that to placate me. Still, I saw day after day how good Bevy felt after an hour of journaling and I figured I'd stop worrying about what she might be saying about me and just focus on the fact that she was happy.

When Fisher was younger and constantly fighting with his father, I handed him one of Bevy's blank journals and urged him to get his thoughts out of his head and onto paper. I told him if he wrote them down, he could close the book and walk away from those troubles, rather than bottling them up and letting them fester. I know Fisher has kept up with his writing through the years and it was one of the most helpful things for him during his year in rehab for PTSD. It makes me feel good knowing he inherited something from Bevy even though he never knew it.

My Bevy and I spent so many years living happily together before everything changed. Why couldn't I be enough for her? Why wasn't my love enough? I'll never understand those men who have such a burning desire to be fathers. I never had that, even after I became one. I loved my son more than I thought possible, but nothing could surpass the love I had for my wife.

If I knew then what I know now and all that other bullshit...I don't even know if I'd have done things differently. How could I? I loved Bevy to distraction and I would have done anything in my power to give her the one thing she wanted. I prayed harder than

I'd ever prayed before and it was a damn miracle God listened to me. Do I regret those prayers I wasted begging God for a baby instead of saving them for something more important further down the road? Sometimes. Most of the time.

It's getting a little harder to breathe and my chest feels tighter than it did when I woke up, but I push through the pain, just like Bevy did when she gave birth to Jefferson. I think back to the night he was conceived, wondering if I should include it in my story. Will Jefferson really want to read about his parents' sex life? Will Fisher be embarrassed to know that his old grandfather was a horny devil when it came to Bevy? Probably, but it's an important part of this tale.

Chapter 13

July 1959

BEVY HASN'T SPOKEN to me for almost two weeks. It's the longest we've ever gone without speaking and it's about to kill me. Each time I try to apologize, she walks right past me with a huff. I'm getting a little tired of sleeping on the couch. I want to be back in bed with my wife. Shoot, at this point I'd take her yelling and cursing at me again over the silent treatment. I know I shouldn't have said what I did to her, but I needed to be honest with Bevy. After seven years of failed pregnancy attempts, I can't take the disappointment on Bevy's face each month anymore. The doctors told us that there's nothing medically wrong with either one of us from what they gather, it's just something that happens–or doesn't happen, in our case.

Even with the doctors flat out telling Bevy that we will most likely never have a child of our own, she won't give up. She still talks about how she'd like to decorate the nursery

WORTH THE TRIP

and she still daydreams about the child that she is so desperate to have. I don't understand her desperation. We have a good life together, just the two of us. Why does she want to ruin it? I don't want to share her with anyone else and it hurts my heart that she doesn't think of it that way. She says that we have enough love to give a hundred children.

After a long day at work helping to build a new restaurant that is going up on Main Street, I walk into our house and the first thing I notice is the eerie quiet. Just like my parents did when I was little, Bevy always has music playing. There's no better welcome home than watching my beautiful bride dancing around the living room, singing like an angel. The silence is unnerving.

I quickly wash the grime off of my hands at the kitchen sink and go in search of Bevy. I find her standing in the spare bedroom, staring out the window.

"Hey, is everything okay?" I ask softly as I move closer to her.

She doesn't turn around or answer me, but I refuse to be ignored anymore. I love her, I want her to be happy and I just need her to understand that.

"Look, Bevy, I'm sorry. I never should

have said the things I did. I just can't take you getting upset month after month. Seeing you get your hopes up and watching your spirit die when you find out we aren't going to have a baby…. I don't want you to go through that anymore. Can you understand how much it's killing me?" I ask as I gently rest my hands on her shoulders and turn her to face me.

There are tears streaming down her cheeks and her face is flushed from the crying she must have been doing for quite a while before I came home.

"Oh, Bevy, my Bevy, please don't cry," I plead as I pull her into my arms.

She puts her hands on my chest and pushes away from me angrily.

"How do you expect me not to cry, Trip? I can't have a baby! WE can't have a baby. My heart is *broken* and you just don't get it. You keep telling me to forget about it and just be happy with what we have, but how am I supposed to do that?" she argues.

I throw my hands up in the air in frustration. "Because we ARE happy! I love you and you love me. You get to teach choir up at the elementary school and do what you love, surrounded by children. Why can't that be enough for you? Why can't what we have

WORTH THE TRIP

together be enough for you?"

"BECAUSE IT'S NOT!" she shouts back. "Those are OTHER PEOPLE'S children, Trip, not ours. They aren't a piece of our heart and soul. They don't have your cocky attitude and my blue eyes. Don't you want someone to carry on our traditions and our family long after we're gone? Don't you want a little piece of you and I combined together walking on this earth? I want that, Trip. I want that so badly that I can hardly breathe with wanting it so much."

She takes a step closer to me and rests her palms over my chest, close to my heart. "I want a piece of this heart, that I love more than anything, to be in another human being. I want to create something beautiful and amazing together and I want you to understand how much it means to me. I want you to understand that I feel like a failure because I can't do this one thing. This one, simple thing that thousands of women do every single day and I can't do it! Why can't I do it?" she cries as the tears start to flow again.

"You are NOT a failure, Bevy. You're my wife, my best friend, a friend to everyone on this island and someone that people look up to because of your strength and determination

95

and fearlessness. I don't understand this because it's turning you into someone I don't know. It's making you sad all the time and it's making you scared," I tell her, grabbing her hands in mine and bringing them up to my lips. I kiss the tops of her hands and then hold them tightly against my chest. "My heart belongs to you and it beats for you and seeing you like this is breaking it in two. Don't you think I feel like a failure, too? I'm letting you down because I just can't make you happy anymore. I can't take away your pain and make things better and it kills me. Tell me how to make this better, Bevy, please."

She pulls one of her hands out from under mine and swipes angrily at the tears on her cheeks. "I don't know, Trip. I don't know how to make this better. I don't know how to make the sadness go away. I don't know how to stop wanting something that I can't have."

"Why can't I be enough for you? Why can't what we have together just be enough?" I ask sadly.

"Oh, Trip. You are more than enough for me. I love you more than I ever thought possible. I love you more today than yesterday. Every day, I'm amazed by how much more I love you, but this is different. This is a different kind of love that I need. I love our life together, but I just need something more. It has nothing to do with not being happy with you or with the life we've built together. I just want to be a mother. I want to prove to myself and everyone else that I can be the kind of mother mine never was. I want a child that I'll never ignore, a child that I'll be proud of, a child that I will make sure knows, every day of his or her life, that they are wanted and loved and cherished."

I've always wondered if Bevy's need to have a child stemmed from her own disastrous childhood and she just confirmed my beliefs. I hate her parents now more than I ever have for the way they ignored her after Benjamin died. Even now, as an adult, her father barely speaks to her. I always thought that when her mother killed herself, her father would finally wake up and realize that life is too short and embrace the only family he had left, but that wasn't the case. He became even more focused on work and pushed Bevy even further away.

I wrap my arms tightly around Bevy's waist and pull her against me. "You would never, EVER be the type of parent that yours were. You have so much love to give, Bevy, and I envy that in you. Any child would be blessed to have you as a mother. I'm sorry I can't give this to you, Bevy. I'm sorry I can't give you the one thing you need."

Bevy sniffles and finally gives me a smile, something I've been desperate to see again for the last few weeks. She leans up on her toes and presses her lips to mine. It's a quick peck on the lips, not nearly enough after not touching her for fourteen days.

"I love you, Trip. I love you and I'm sorry I've been such a rotten wife. You give me more than I need and I'm sorry for making you feel like it's not enough."

I squeeze her tighter and my heart beats faster as her fingers slide through the hair at my nape. I press my forehead to hers and let out a deep sigh.

"You could never be a rotten wife, even if you tried, Bevy," I reassure her.

She slides out of my arms and grabs my hands, pulling me out of the spare room and across the hall to our bedroom. Bevy has never been shy when it comes to lovemaking, but the speed with which she removes her clothes and helps me remove mine before pushing me backwards onto the bed renders me speechless. I clutch her hips tightly as she crawls on top of me and leans her body over mine, her hair making a curtain around our faces.

"I've missed you, Trip. I've missed you so much," she whispers.

Making love to my wife is always amazing, but this time it's so much more. We move together quickly, almost desperately. We clutch tightly to each other and whisper words of love as we reconnect in the best possible way. I love the feel of her around me and the sounds she makes, letting me know that she feels as deeply as I do. I love everything about this woman in my arms and I tell her so as she moves on top of me, bringing us both the release that we need to wash away the sadness and the regrets. I hold her tighter than ever, I love her stronger than before and pray to God that he will give Bevy the one thing she needs more than me to mend her wounded heart.

Chapter 14

I SET MY pen down and take a moment to close my eyes and remember the day that our son was conceived. God answered my prayers that day, and even though I was scared shitless when we found out Bevy was pregnant, I was happy that she'd finally gotten her wish. I'd never seen her smile so big, laugh so hard or be so filled with joy as she was during those nine months before he was born. Her excitement was infectious, and even though I wasn't so sure about what kind of father I would be, I threw myself wholeheartedly into preparing for the birth of our son. I painted the nursery, I built a crib and a changing table and I walked around with my chest puffed out, proud of the fact that I was finally able to make Bevy's dreams come true.

Jefferson Junior showed up a week early and Bevy gave birth at home with Doc Wilson and my mother by her side and me pacing like a mad man out in the hallway, listening to her cries of pain and wishing I could take them away.

WORTH THE TRIP

I open my eyes and stare at a photo of Bevy in bed, looking radiant with baby Jefferson curled up in her arms just minutes after he was born. She's running the tips of her fingers over his chubby little cheek and smiling down at him with such love and devotion. I remember being so relieved that he arrived safely and so proud that Bevy had done something so incredibly difficult and amazing. She grew a life inside of her and brought him into this world all on her own. I also remember feeling a twinge of jealousy when I snapped this photo. All of the love and devotion that had belonged solely to me would now be transferred to someone else. I hated myself for feeling that way, but I couldn't make it stop no matter how hard I tried.

I should have loved him more. I should have cherished all of the parts of him that were so clearly Bevy, but I couldn't do it. Years later, once she was gone, I couldn't handle anything that reminded me of her. With his curly brown hair and bright blue eyes and his infectious laugh, he was my Bevy made over and it hurt to even look at him. I should have done better for my son. I should have honored Bevy's memory by loving him as much as she did, I just didn't know how.

101

For too many years, I blamed Jefferson for what happened to Bevy. In my grief, I couldn't separate that precious little boy from the monster that stole the love of my life. Every time I thought about how I would never hear her voice or touch her face again, all of the reasons why led back to Jefferson. I hate myself for the way I behaved then.

Tearing the pages I've already written on out of the notepad, I set them aside and start on a clean page. I glance out the window and see that the sun has disappeared and there are ugly, dark clouds hovering over the water. There's a storm brewing and I should probably get up and check on my family, but I need to finish this. The hardest part of my story is coming up next and I need to get through it. I'm starting to feel sick to my stomach and I'm not sure if it's because of the horrible memories floating around in my head or because there is something seriously wrong with me. Rubbing my fist against my chest, I try to soothe the shooting pain, but it doesn't help. Just a little bit more. I only have a little bit more to write and then I can go check on everyone and make sure they're safe.

With a shaking hand, I press the pen to the paper and a little part of me dies inside as

WORTH THE TRIP

I relive the worst time of my life.

I lose a piece of myself every time I think back on that day. Pretty soon, there will be nothing left.

Chapter 15

October 1965

"WE BELIEVE THE cancer has been growing since Beverly gave birth to Jefferson Junior. Her uterus went through so much trauma during the delivery that it was susceptible to the disease," the doctor explains.

I shake my head in denial. It can't be possible. Jefferson turned five years old in April. Five years since he was born and she's had this *thing* growing inside of her, slowly killing her?

Bevy has been sick off and on ever since Jefferson was born, but we never thought it could possibly be something so serious. For four years, I've watched my wife battle cold after flu after pneumonia, and the doctors always told us she just had a low immune system. Plenty of rest, plenty of liquids, that was always the magic cure. When she fainted the other morning and I couldn't wake her up, I rushed her to the doctor and he finally ran some tests.

"What do we do? How do we fix it?" I ask.

The specialist who Doc Wilson brought over from the mainland pats me on the back and shakes his head sadly.

"There's nothing we can do, Mr. Fisher. I'm sorry, but your wife has stage four stomach cancer. We believe it started in her uterus and traveled through her body. All we can do right now is make her comfortable for the little time she has left."

I stare down the hall of our home at the closed bedroom door where Bevy is resting. Glancing around the room at the framed photos of our life together, I want to rip them from the walls and let them shatter on the floor so they resemble the pile of rubble that is my heart. She promised she wouldn't leave me. All those years ago on that beach when I finally gathered up the courage to tell her how I felt and asked her to marry me, she promised she wouldn't leave. She's going to leave me here alone, in this house we built together, in this life we *live* together.

I turn away from the doctor and run from the house. He shouts after me and both of my parents call my name as I race past them on the front porch. They came over this morning to keep Jefferson occupied while I spoke with the doctors, and even though I'm thankful for their help, I can't talk to them right now. I can't talk to anyone. I want to scream and cry and punch holes in the walls, not watch my parents fall apart when they find out the news.

Getting into my car, I crank up the engine and peel out of the driveway, leaving my parents and Jefferson standing on the front porch looking after me worriedly. I don't know where to go, I don't know what to do. When I have a problem, I talk it out with Bevy. Whenever I'm in need of advice, I go to Bevy. I can't very well go to Bevy and ask her how I'm supposed to live without her, can I?

Ten minutes later, I find myself pulling into the cemetery. I haven't been back here since the day of the funeral and I feel guilty, but I know he'd forgive me. Parking my car alongside the path that will take me to the grave with the small American flag stuck into the ground in front of it, I get out of the car and walk towards the headstone. I squat down in front of it and busy myself brushing leaves and freshly mowed grass off the top of it.

Staring at the etching, I trace my fingers over the letters.

Billy "Kid" Fortney
June 2, 1932 – July 21, 1965
Son, Friend, Hero, Marine

My best friend was killed in Vietnam a few months ago. When Kennedy became president and there was talk of sending US troops to aid South Vietnam, that idiot went and joined the Marines. He was too old to be drafted when the time came, but that fool had to go and volunteer, still dreaming of being a gun-toting outlaw and finding a way to do it legally. He was with the first group of 3,500 Marines sent to Vietnam back in March and the dumbass stepped on a landmine. He spent nearly two decades counseling me over Beverly O'Bryne Fisher, and I feel sure he'd know exactly what to say right now. I miss him more now than I did when I first found out he was gone.

"I'm going to lose her, Billy. I don't know what the hell to do. How do I live without her?"

I can almost hear him calling me all sorts of names for being an idiot. I know I'm behaving irrationally and that running away was not my best decision. I should have gone right to Bevy, held her in my arms and told her everything was going to be okay, but lying is something I've never been capable of with that woman. That's why I had to get out of that house. Nothing is going to be okay ever again.

I sit down in the grass with my back against the headstone and I have a nice, long talk with my best friend. I tell him how scared I am, I tell him how unfair it is and I tell him I wish it were me going through this instead of her. The wind rustles my hair and I imagine it's Billy telling me to stop being a jackass and go to her.

By the time I return to the house, the doctors are gone and my mother has taken Jefferson back to my parents' home for the night. My father rocks back and forth on the front porch and I sit with him for a few minutes in silence before he speaks.

"Whatever you need, son, it's yours. You need to us to take Jefferson for a while, your mother and I would be more than happy," he tells me before pushing himself up from the rocker and walking down the steps.

My father and I aren't the most emotion-ally expressive people, but his words mean more to me than he'll ever know. I can't even think about taking care of Jefferson right now. We spent seven years trying to bring him into this world and at the time, it felt like a blessing from God that Bevy was finally able to get pregnant. Now, the idea of raising him on my own scares me to death. I don't know the first thing about taking care of a child. Bevy has been perfectly content doing everything on her own and shooing me away when I offer to help. I've played catch with him out in the yard, I've taken him fishing and started teaching him how to ride a bike – all of the typical things a father is supposed to do with his son – but I have no idea what the hell else raising a child entails. Bevy can't leave me, she just can't.

Getting up from the chair, I slowly make my way down the hall and into our bedroom. Bevy is propped up in bed with a bunch of pillows behind her. Her eyes are closed and as much as I know she needs her rest, I need to hear her voice more. I need her reassurance that everything will be okay. She's the one dying and I'm the one who needs comfort – I realize how selfish that sounds, I really do, but I can't bring myself to care.

I carefully climb into bed with Bevy and

wrap my arms around her waist, resting my head on her chest. I feel her arms come around me, and a few seconds later, her fingers slide over and over through my hair.

"I'm so sorry, Trip," she whispers.

I squeeze my eyes closed and hold onto her tighter. Maybe if I hold on tight enough, she won't leave.

"You have nothing to be sorry about, Bevy," I tell her.

"I promised I'd never leave you and now I'm breaking that promise."

A tear escapes from my eyes and drops down onto her cotton nightgown. I let go of her long enough to brush it away, and then I push myself up on my hands so I can look down at her.

"I love you, Bevy, and I'm telling you, you have nothing to be sorry about. It's going to be okay, everything is going to be okay."

I smile, even though every lie cuts me like a knife, and she smiles back at me, even though she knows I'm lying. Nothing will ever be okay again.

Her hands come up to cup my face and she stares into my eyes. "You're going to be okay, Trip. You are the strongest man I know, and you're going to be okay."

I don't answer her. I don't tell her that each second I live with the knowledge that we won't be growing old together, I feel like the weakest person in the world. I lay my head on the pillow next to her and she curls her body into mine. I memorize the smell of her skin and how it feels to have her warm breath puffing over my chest. I think about every moment we've spent together since we were children. Every laugh, every smile, every kiss, every tear and every argument. I remember the good times and I remember the bad times, flipping through them in my mind like a slideshow. In this moment, listening to Bevy breathe and feeling the weight of her body next to mine, I make a silent promise that I will never forget a single moment I've spent with her.

"Hey, Trip, I'll race you to heaven," Bevy says with a halfhearted chuckle.

I try to stifle my sob as I brush her hair out of her eyes and stare at her beautiful face lying next to me on the pillow.

"You always have to win, don't you Bevy?" I reply as the tears roll down my cheeks.

"Always," she says with a smile.

"I love you."

"I love you more," she replies easily.

"Just remember who said it first," I tell her as she closes her eyes and drifts off to sleep.

Chapter 16

MY BEVY DIED on a Tuesday, four weeks, three days and twenty hours after we found out she had cancer. She'd grown restless in bed at night, so I'd taken to sleeping on a chair next to our bed. I opened my eyes with the morning sun and she had her back to me. I stretched the kinks out of my neck and back and called her name, but she didn't answer me. Bevy died peacefully in her sleep, the way everyone should go. She went to bed with a smile on her face, telling me she loved me, and never woke up.

We buried her on a Saturday and it would be almost a year before I emerged from our home. I shut down and I closed myself off. I realized I was behaving exactly how Bevy's mother did when Benjamin died and I was disgusted with my behavior, but there was nothing I could do to change it. I barely ate, I hardly slept and I couldn't muster up the emotion to care what was happening to my son. My parents took Jefferson home with them after the funeral and I was so consumed by my own grief that I didn't bother checking on my own flesh and blood at any point during that entire year. What that poor little boy must have been feeling tears a hole right through my heart. His mother was his whole world. True to her word, she was NEVER like her parents. She loved that little boy with all of her heart and soul and made sure he knew it every day. She showered him with kisses and tickles and she was constantly telling him that she wished for him all of her life and that God answering her prayers was the best gift she could have ever been given. I was a fool for believing Bevy's heart wasn't big enough for the both of us. She had more than enough love to go around and she proved that every day until she drew her last breath.

I'm not proud of the way I behaved. I should have told Jefferson about the remarkable woman who gave him life long before now. Even when my mother brought Jefferson to visit with me after I crawled out of the black hole of grief and depression, I never spoke of Bevy. I never said her name and I certainly never shared stories about her life. Pretending she never existed was the only way I was able get up and put one foot in front of the other every morning. The only way I was able to breathe was to push her from my mind. If I thought about her, if I remembered the love we shared for just one second, I would crumble to the floor and pray for death, just to be with her again. I don't know how many times during that first year I held a gun to my head after downing a bottle of whiskey and just wished I could end the pain. Every damn time, I'd see Bevy's angry face in my mind, the guilt kicked in and I'd lose my nerve.

All I can think of now is how much I let Bevy down. Our son deserved to know how wild and rambunctious she was as a child and how strong and amazing she was as a woman. I should have kept her memory alive and spoke about her each and every day. If the tables were turned, Bevy wouldn't have allowed Jefferson to go through life not knowing what kind of person I was. I left my son, the last piece of my Bevy on this earth, to be raised by someone else. He lost both of his parents the day Bevy died and there aren't enough words in the English language to erase that fact, but maybe reading my story will help him understand.

All these years later, he doesn't need me,

he doesn't want me and I'm not even sure that he loves me. He looks at me like I'm a stranger, and I am. Because of my father's influence, he became a strong, successful businessman. My father took him to the bank every day, grooming *my* son to take over the role that *his* never wanted. Jefferson thrived under his grandfather's tutelage and it didn't seem right, when I finally got my shit together, to take away the only source of stability he'd had since his mother left us. My father tried, as did my mother, to make me wake up and realize that I was losing my son, the only part of Bevy I had left, but at that point, it was too late. The damage was done.

Looking at one of the few photos I have of Jefferson when he was a young boy, I'm overcome with feelings of grief and loss. The two of us are standing in front of a half-built structure, me covered in dirt and grime and little Jefferson looking sharp in a nicely pressed suit. I'm helping him hold a hammer and he looks so adorably uncomfortable that I don't know whether to laugh or cry because this photo was taken the day I realized I'd probably lost him forever.

And it was my own fault.

Chapter 17

April 1967

HAMMERING THE LAST nail into the board, I take a step back and stare up at the building in front of me, proud of what I've accomplished. These last few months, being outside in the sunshine instead of drunk and cooped up inside the house, have been good for me. When my father stopped by and told me they needed a general manager to oversee the construction of a new bed and breakfast on the southern end of the island, I dragged my ass out of bed and forced myself to go to work. The distraction has been good for me. It's kept my mind off the whiskey in my kitchen cabinet calling my name, and instead of looking sickly and pale all the time, I've got a nice, golden tan from all the hours spent working outside. I still feel like death most of the time and it's always an effort to get out of bed first thing in the morning, but I have to do it. I can't keep going on the way I have for the past year.

"Trip! The inn is looking wonderful!"

I turn to see my mother standing a few feet behind me, smiling in awe at the huge building.

Pulling a rag out of the back pocket of my jeans, I wipe the sweat from my head and walk towards her. It's then that I notice someone behind her, hiding behind her long skirt. My heart thumps in my chest and part of me wants to turn and run away. I'm not ready for this. I can't handle this, not right now, not when I've finally got my shit together.

My mother sees the panic on my face and gives me a reassuring smile, reaching behind her and tugging the little person out in front of her. My breath catches in my lungs when I get my first good look at him in almost a year. He's got a full head of curly brown hair that my mother has cut short and his blue eyes are so much like *hers* that my legs threaten to give out from under me.

"Jefferson, say hello to your father," my mother urges.

He gives me a shy smile and I feel tears forming in my eyes. Two dimples, one in each cheek, just like his mother. It's too much. It *hurts* too much.

"Whatcha doin'?" he asks in a quiet voice as he looks at the building behind me.

I swallow thickly, unable to form any words to answer him. He's so small and beautiful and his voice warms my cold heart, even though it's so painful to hear.

"Your daddy is building an inn so that guests can spend the night here on the island, isn't that wonderful, Jefferson? Your daddy is very talented," my mother brags, giving me a big smile. "Does the inn have a name yet?"

I finally tear my eyes away from my son to look at my mother. "Butler House Inn. It's called Butler House Inn. It should be finished in another month or so."

She smiles and nods, giving Jefferson a gentle shove on the back to move him closer to me. "I have a few errands to run. I thought it would be nice if you two spent some time together."

Without giving me a chance to protest, she bends down and kisses Jefferson on the cheek, telling him she loves him and that she'll be back for him soon.

She quickly walks away and Jefferson and I stand there, quietly staring at each other. I don't know what the hell to do. I don't know what to say. Does he even *want* to spend time with me? I didn't realize until now how much I've missed him and how horrible of a father I've been. I more or less washed my hands of him, leaving the childrearing to my parents, not bothering to ask about him or attempt to see him. This little boy doesn't even know me, and that thought is suddenly very sad.

Jefferson takes a few tentative steps towards me before reaching out towards the hammer I still have clutched tightly in my hand.

"What's that?" he asks me as he stares at it curiously.

I turn the hammer over in my hand and squat down to his level. "Um, this is a hammer. It's what I used to build that big building behind me. Do you want to try and use it?"

He scrunches up his face and I can just see the wheels turning in his mind. He finally shrugs and holds his hand out to me. I place the hammer in his hand and chuckle when the weight of it makes his arm drop and the hammer smacks into the ground.

"Did I break it?" he asks worriedly.

I laugh again, reaching out and wrapping my large hands around his small ones to help him lift it back up.

"Nope, you didn't break it, it's just a little heavy. How about I teach you how to use this thing? Do you want to hit a few nails into some wood?"

He shrugs again and I stand up, holding my hand out for him to take. My heart stutters when he slides his soft, clean hand into my callused, dirty one. I walk him over to a pile of scrap wood and show him how to hold the nail against the wood and gently hammer at it to get it started. It takes a few tries for him to get the hang of holding the nail steady while moving the hammer, but with my help, we get a few nails pounded into the remnant piece of wood.

"Well, would you look at that?" I tell him as we both stand back and admire the work. "You're a natural with a hammer."

Jefferson hands the hammer back to me and shoves his hands into the front pocket of his pants.

"Did you know Papa owns a bank?" Jefferson asks with a huge, excited smile on his face. "He takes me there almost every day. I get to count money and go into the big vault and look at all the coins. I like going to the bank."

I try to smile at the happiness in his voice,

but it's hard. I know he's only a child and it's not like I've made any effort to steer my son towards the craft that I love, but hearing him talk about having fun at the damn bank almost breaks my heart. It's my own fault for not bringing him to a construction site or letting him play with my tools. It was my job to teach him how amazing it is to build something with your own two hands. I'm happy that my father dotes on him and teaches him things, but I'm sad that my son doesn't share the same enthusiasm for my work.

"Did you know I'm the manager for the construction of this building?" I ask him as we turn and look at the structure behind us. "I've told everyone where each and every board goes and where all the nails need to be hammered. I get to be outside in the sun every day, building something."

Jefferson shields his eyes from the sun as he stares up at the inn with a bored expression on his face.

"Your hands and your shirt are dirty," he suddenly says.

I look down at myself, feeling a little ashamed that I'm covered in dirt and sweat the first time my son is seeing me in almost a

WORTH THE TRIP

year.

"Yep, that's what happens when you do what I do. You never stay clean," I tell him with a shrug.

"I get to dress up when I go to the bank with Papa. Nana bought me a new suit and a bunch of different colored ties and she even taught me how to tie them. Papa said when I'm older, I can have my very own office with a desk and a secretary who will get me coffee."

I laugh out loud at his exuberance in spite of my jealousy.

"My birthday was last week. I'm seven now."

My laughter dies quickly in my throat and tears prickle the back of my eyes. "I know, buddy. I'm so sorry I missed it."

Resting my hand on his tiny shoulder, I bend back down so I'm eye-level with him. "How about we take a break and go into town for some ice cream to celebrate. Do you want chocolate chip or strawberry?"

Jefferson's eyes light up and he smiles the biggest smile I've ever seen. "I LOVE chocolate chip! But I have to make sure to use napkins and not wipe my face on my sleeve. I'm going to the bank with Papa later, and I

123

don't want to be dirty."

I choke back my tears and nod at him before taking his hand in mine again.

Chapter 18

TRIED, BUT by that point it was too late. One year of absence from my son's life was enough for another man to come in and be a better father figure to him than I could ever hope to be. The relationship with my parents became strained after that. I wanted my son back home with me, but he didn't want to come. In the end, I chose to do what was best for him. After that day at Butler House Inn, I went to see him as often as I could and I tried to show him how fun it was to use tools and work with your hands, but I eventually had to accept the fact that my son would never be a craftsman. Jefferson's heart and mind were set on a fancy office where a pretty woman brought you coffee and where you never got dirty or sweaty.

My son wasn't always a pompous ass with nothing but money on the brain. Once upon a time, he was a sweet, innocent little boy whose father abandoned him. Over the years, even though he didn't want to live with me, he grew to resent the fact that I didn't come for him right after Bevy died. He hated me a little more each time I refused to talk about his mother or answer questions about our life together. Before I could even blink, he was a grown man, getting married and starting a family of his own.

The day my grandson was born was one of the most bittersweet days of my life. The sweet woman Jefferson married is the only reason I was allowed to have a relationship with Fisher. She knew Jefferson and I had a strained relationship and she didn't want any part of that to touch her son. In a way, Fisher became more like a son to me than my own. I gave all of my love and attention to him as a way to make up for not giving it to his father. I taught him how to work with wood and instilled in him a love of creating something out of nothing. I made him see that doing what made him happy was the only way to live.

Fisher was a way for me to make amends for my past and maybe doting on him more than I did my own son was the wrong thing to do, but it was the only thing I *could* do. He was my second chance at getting it right and I vowed not to screw things up with him. Seeing my son repeat my mistakes with Fisher made me angry, though I certainly had no right to be. Jefferson doesn't understand unconditional love for his child and only wanting what's best for him because I never gave that to *him*. I was the catalyst to all of the things that went wrong with this family and I will bear that guilt forever.

I want Jefferson to understand. I NEED him to understand. I wanted to be a better father, I wanted to love him to distraction like Bevy did, just as she'd made me promise before she died, but I didn't know how. I wasted an entire year of his life so lost in my own sadness and figuring out how I was going to go on that I didn't consider how it might be affecting him.

A gust of wind blows around the house and I hear it creak and moan in protest. Looking out the window, I see that the dark clouds hovering overhead have opened up and it looks like something bad has arrived on Fisher's Island. Leaning over to the transistor radio sitting on the end table next to the couch, I flip it on and listen to the warnings of an approaching hurricane. I can barely feel my left arm now. It's grown numb over last few hours and I'm thankful that I'm right-handed and don't need it to write. There's one last thing I have to take care of.

Tearing off a clean sheet of paper while the wind howls and the rain beats against the windows, I compose a letter to my son, telling him everything he deserved to know years ago. I speak from the heart and I hope that he'll read it and understand. I hope that he'll forgive me.

Chapter 19

Dear Jefferson:

By the time you read this, I'll probably be gone. I'm not feeling so well and I know my time is coming. I should be afraid because of all the things I've done and all the things I've left unsaid, but I'm not. I hope you've read the words I've written down in these pages. I'm sorry I never shared these things with you before now. I should have been a better man. I should have been a better father. There are a lot of things I should have done differently where you were concerned and I hope you can understand, even if you can't forgive me.

You don't always get everything you want out of life. Sometimes you do, but then they're ripped out of your hands before you're ready. I wasn't ready to lose your mother. I don't think I ever would have been ready, even if she'd lived to be a hundred years old. She was my light in the darkness, my reason for living and my best friend. I should have taken a page out of her book and realized that there was enough love in my heart for more than just her. I did love you, son. I DO love you. I'm proud of you, even though I think you're being a complete ass where Fisher is concerned. I'm going to tell you what your grandmother said to me a long time ago: Get your head out of your ass and look at what's right in front of you.

Okay, so she didn't use those exact words, but you catch my drift.

Jefferson, you have an amazing son. A son who is a hero and a fighter and loves with everything inside of him. Cherish that boy and be thankful that you created such an amazing man. He's a part of you, and you should be proud of who he's become. Stop being hung up on the fact that he didn't want to follow in your footsteps. I didn't follow in my father's and you certainly didn't follow in mine. We all have to make our own paths in life and the only thing that matters is that we're happy with the trail we walk. Fisher is happy, can you see that? Lucy makes him happy, building things makes him happy, living each day to the fullest makes him happy. Be happy for him, Jefferson. Embrace the daughter-in-law that gives light to his darkness, just as your mother did for me. I promise, you don't want to realize too late that you've made mistakes. There's no going back, no matter how hard you try. I made so many mistakes with you and I wish every day that I could fix them. Be the father that I never knew how to be. Love your son like I never knew how to love you until it was too late and you didn't need me anymore.

The only thing that scares me about dying is going to my grave with a son who hates me. I hope you understand the things I did more clearly now. I have to accept the path that *I* chose and I have to walk this final trail alone, and that's on me, not you. The best parts of you, the thoughtful, sweet, beautiful, kindhearted parts that I know are in there somewhere – those are all your mother. Honor her memory by finding those parts. Share those parts with your wife and your son and your daughter-in-law and the grandchildren that I know they'll give you. Lucy and Fisher remind me so much of your mother and I. They love each other to distraction. It's the only way to love, my son. Love them to distraction. Love every part of them and don't go another day without telling them that. Be kind, be happy and be thankful for the blessings you've been given in life.

I love you, Jefferson. I'm sorry. Please forgive me.

Your Father

Chapter 20

MY BRAIN IS fuzzy and everything hurts. I know I'm lying on the floor, but I can't seem to open my eyes to figure out why. I can hear people shouting, someone crying and screaming for a doctor, and the wind and rain battering the house. I want to tell them to stop worrying and that everything is okay. The pain is so bad that I don't even care what happens to me now. I just want to go. I want to go where there is no pain, where my heart no longer hurts and I can live without regret. Someone is clutching my hand and telling me to hang on just a little bit longer. I open my mouth to tell them I just can't do it anymore. I've hung on far longer than I wanted to. I don't know where I'm going, but I'm ready. I want to be free. Please, just let me be free.

I SLOWLY OPEN my eyes and the first thing I

WORTH THE TRIP

notice is how bright it is. I squint until I get used to the light and then blink a few times to bring my eyes into focus. Reaching up, I rest my hand against my chest and realize it doesn't hurt any longer. As a matter of fact, nothing hurts. I feel like I could run a hundred miles, I have so much energy. I want to jump up and down, but an eighty-three-year old man can still break a hip, no matter how good he feels. Looking around me, I realize I'm on the beach, down by the lighthouse, and I have no idea how I got here. The last thing I remember was going over to Butler House to check on Lucy and her guests. She ran out of the house into the storm to go find Fisher and while I was screaming after her to get her ass back inside, I felt myself falling.

When the hell did I wake up and walk down to the lighthouse?

The sun is shining bright and the waves gently roll up onto the shore. There are no signs of the horrible storm that came to the island earlier and it makes me wonder what's going on. I look up and I don't find a cloud in the sky for as far as the eye can see. The sand is dry as a bone and there isn't any debris littering the beach like there should be after a hurricane.

Jesus, how long was I out?

I start strolling along the beach, enjoying the nice weather and trying to get my jumbled thoughts in order, when I hear a voice in the distance. I stop walking and tilt my head to the side to try and hear better. The voice sounds again and chills skate up my spine. I know that voice. That soft, sweet, melodic voice that has filled my dreams for too many years to count. I must have hit my head when I fell, that's the only explanation. I hit my head and now I've lost my damn mind. I squeeze my eyes closed and will that voice away, even though it's the only sound I want to hear.

"Trip. Trip, over here!"

I try not to cry when the voice sounds like it's coming from right behind me, so close I could reach out and touch the person it belongs to.

"Open your eyes, my love."

I let out a sob as I open my eyes to a sight I refuse to believe. She's not really here. She's not standing right in front of me with her long, curly hair and big blue eyes and a beautiful smile on her face as she looks up at me.

"It's about damn time, Trip Fisher," she says with a laugh.

WORTH THE TRIP

I let out a shaky breath and slowly reach my hand out towards her.

"Are you real?" I ask in a whisper.

She grabs my hand and presses it to her cheek. "As real as the sand you're standing on and the ocean at our backs."

Bevy gives me another big smile and I shake my head back and forth in denial.

"How is this happening? How are you here?"

She drops my hand, takes a step towards me and cups my face in her hands. "We're here together, Trip. We're finally here together."

She looks exactly like she did fifty years ago. Her skin is smooth and young and her hair is the same chocolate brown shade it had been since it darkened up when she was a teenager. There aren't any wrinkles around her eyes, there aren't any age spots on her hands and she moves with fluidity and grace, unlike my old, decrepit self. I suddenly feel self-conscious, and as much as I want to pull her into my arms and never let go, I take a step back. I'm an old man now, an old man who's lived fifty years without her. I've aged and I've changed. I'm not the same handsome young man she fell in love with. I look every

135

bit my eight-three-years of age when she doesn't look a day over thirty-one, the age she was when she died.

"Trip, what's wrong?" she asks.

I shake my head back and forth in shame for being so vain. "You're so young and beautiful. You're exactly how I remembered you, how I've dreamed of you. I'm not...I don't..."

I trail off and tear my gaze away from hers so she doesn't see the tears pooling in my eyes. It's not fair that the first time I get to see her again, it has to be like this. At the end of my life as an old man.

Bevy suddenly laughs, and even though I'm sad, it's like music to my ears. My eyes find hers and she shakes her head at me.

"Oh, Trip, you silly man. Look. Turn around," she instructs me as she grabs onto my shoulders and turns me away from her.

Standing in the sand right behind us is a huge mirror. I have no idea how it got there and I don't care because the reflection in front of me takes my breath away. It's me, but it's not me. The man in the mirror can't be more than thirty-something. He's got brown, slicked back hair instead of a head of white, old man hair. He's got smooth skin and muscles under his t-shirt that haven't withered away. I tear my gaze away from the mirror to look down at my hands. The age spots and wrinkles have been replaced with strong, young hands. I run those young hands over my face and find the same results. I quickly turn away from the mirror to look at Bevy in confusion.

"I'm not old. How am I not old?" I ask her.

She smiles again and runs her hand down the side of my face. "There's no age here, Trip. There's nothing but happiness. You can be whoever you want to be. You can be whatever age you want to be. When you got here, you must have been thinking about this age and that's why it happened. You're still just as handsome as ever."

I laugh through my tears and finally pull her into my arms. She still smells like flowers and my heart still beats in triple time when I feel her this close to me.

"I'm sorry, Bevy. I'm sorry it took me so long to get here," I whisper in her ear.

She pulls back and looks into my eyes. "I'm the one who's sorry, Trip. Time here, it's different than anywhere else. For me, it was only a blink of an eye before you were here. You're the one who had to go through all that time on your own. I'm sorry I left you."

"I'm sorry for so many things, Bevy. I'm sorry for all the time I wasted before I realized I loved you, I'm sorry for not being a better father to our son, I'm sorry for missing you so much that I didn't want to live anymore, I'm sorry—"

Her hand comes up to my mouth and she silences me.

"Shhhh, Trip, it's okay. None of that matters now. You haven't had it easy, my love, and there's nothing to be sorry for. You're here now, we're together and nothing else matters."

Leaning forward, I rest my forehead against hers and sigh contentedly.

"There are so many things I need to tell you. So much has happened, Bevy."

She turns her face up to mine and kisses me softly on the lips. "We have plenty of time for all of that. We have eternity, Trip."

Bevy pulls away and grabs onto my hand, leading me down the beach. "I have something I want to show you."

The smile on her face is contagious and I find myself smiling and laughing right along with her as we race across the sand. I didn't know my legs could still work like this and I feel happier than I've ever been with the ocean breeze rushing through my hair and Bevy's hand in my own.

We get to the end of the beach and begin to climb up a rocky hill. When we get to the top, Bevy points down on the other side. "Look. Look at what you've made possible."

I turn away from her and stare in wonder at the scene at the bottom of the hill. A little boy and a little girl sit side-by-side, playing in the sand together. The little girl looks so much like Bevy with her long, curly hair and blue eyes that I almost think I'm looking into the past at the two of us playing together when we were children. The little boy turns his face, however, and even though he looks familiar, I know it's not me.

"Who are they?" I whisper.

"Just watch," Bevy tells me.

We stand together hand-in-hand, watching the children play. A few minutes later, someone comes up behind them and I smile.

"Little Miss Beverly, look at how dirty your dress is!"

The little girl looks up at Jefferson with his hands on his hips, trying to look stern, but unable to hide the grin on his face.

"Papa!" she squeals as she jumps up from the sand and throws herself into his arms.

He hugs her tightly and twirls her around in the sand until she's giggling so loudly that I can't help but join in.

Bevy leans close to me and rests her head on my shoulder. "That's our great-granddaughter, Beverly. Named after me, of course."

Bevy and I laugh as we continue watching.

"And Mister Trip, are you the one getting my granddaughter all dirty this morning?" Jefferson asks the little boy.

Trip grins up at him and pushes himself up from the sand. "It wasn't my idea, it was Bevy's. She wanted to play in the sand, but I tried to tell her not to get dirty."

"He's lying, Papa! It was all HIS idea!" Beverly argues, her little bow-shaped mouth turning down into a pout.

Jefferson ruffles Trip's hair and holds his hand out for the little boy while he tightens his grip on Beverly in his arms.

"You two bicker like a little old married couple!" Jefferson says with a laugh. "Come on, let's get you guys cleaned up before your parents see."

Jefferson starts walking towards a house that I didn't even notice before now, a little yellow cottage right on the water. Just then, the front door opens and I see Fisher and Lucy walk outside and smile at Jefferson.

"Dad, thanks for wrangling up these two little troublemakers," Fisher tells him with a laugh as he takes his daughter from my son's arms.

"Beverly Ann, how did you already get your dress dirty?" Lucy asks with a chuckle as she gives Jefferson a kiss on the cheek and he wraps his arms around her in a quick hug.

"It was Trip's fault!" Beverly replies indignantly, pointing down at the little boy still clutching Jefferson's hand.

Lucy and Fisher move out of the doorway as another couple steps out onto the porch. Bobby and Ellie share a look before turning their gaze on the little boy.

"Trip, are you causing trouble again?" Bobby asks him as he squats down in font of the boy.

"No, Daddy, I swear! I'm being good, just like always," Trip replies with a smile.

Everyone laughs as Bobby scoops little Trip into his arms and they all move into the house together, Jefferson patting Fisher on the back as they trail in last. When the door closes, I shake my head in disbelief.

"Bobby and Ellie named their son after you, isn't that nice?" Bevy asks. "I have a feeling those four are going to have their hands full with little Bevy and Trip, what do you think?"

I turn to face Bevy and pull her into my arms. "I can't believe it. I just can't believe it. How is this possible? How did we just see that?"

She smiles at me, her hands sliding up my chest before clasping together behind my neck. "I told you, time moves differently here, Trip. A blink of an eye for us is years for everyone else. Our great-granddaughter and Bobby and Ellie's son are both five years old now. Jefferson and our daughter-in-law spend so much time at Fisher and Lucy's house that Fisher jokes about building them a house right next door. Thanks to you, Butler House Inn is thriving better than ever and I have it on good authority that little Miss Beverly is going to be a big sister soon."

I can't erase the look of awe and wonder from my face after what I just witnessed. Lucy and Fisher have a beautiful little girl they

WORTH THE TRIP

named after my Bevy, and Bobby and Ellie have a handsome young son they named after me. Most surprising of all was seeing Jefferson with them, happy and relaxed and full of love for everyone around him and hearing that he spends as much time as possible with his family.

"Full circle, my love. Full circle," Bevy tells me.

"That it is, my Bevy. That it is."

We clasp hands and turn away from the little yellow cottage, heading back down to the beach.

"I need to ask you something serious, Bevy," I tell her as we continue walking.

"No, I won't let you win a race. I already beat you to heaven, I believe that makes me the grand champion of races forever and ever," she says with a laugh, tilting her face up to mine.

Her laughter is contagious and I find myself laughing right along with her until I remember what I wanted to ask her.

"All of those journals you wrote, year after year... Be honest, you were a little bit disappointed that you stayed on the island with me and never got to be a famous singer, weren't you?"

143

I don't know why this is so important to me. I've died and gone to heaven, literally. I have the love of my life at my side once again and from the looks of it, our family is going to be just fine. Now that we have all of eternity stretched out in front of us, I just want to know the truth, once and for all, so I can stop wondering.

"You never read my journals?" she asks in shock.

I shake my head.

"Wow, I'd have definitely read yours if you went first."

I laugh. "It's a good thing I never kept journals, then. Or died first," I laugh.

It feels strange joking about something that haunted me and tortured me for fifty years, but the pain in my heart is gone. The misery of losing her and living without her simply isn't there anymore. I remember each of those fifty years, but it doesn't hurt like it did before. I feel nothing but happiness.

Bevy suddenly stops walking and turns to face me.

"Close your eyes," she tells me.

I close them, but lift one eyelid just enough to peek at her.

"I said close them, Trip Fisher!" she scolds

WORTH THE TRIP

with a laugh, smacking me lightly in the chest.

"Hey, I just had a heart attack, don't hit me in the chest!" I complain with a chuckle, but do as she says.

Bevy grabs both of my hands and gives them a squeeze just as a breeze floats over my face. In seconds, I can clearly see every word contained within her journals floating behind my eyelids. Each passage corresponds with a memory from our time together and they play out like scenes in my mind, but it's the words she wrote the day after we got married that stand out the most.

> "I knew I'd never make it as a singer in California, but it was never really my dream. My dream was always the man sitting on the couch across from me, reading the morning paper. My dream was always Trip Fisher. I told him I was leaving, hoping that he would chase me. And he did."

I open my eyes to find Bevy looking at me with her head tilted to the side and a soft smile on her face.

"I just wanted you to chase me, Trip Fisher."

"I would chase you anywhere, Beverly Fisher," I reply.

Bevy suddenly lets go of my hands and takes off running down the beach, shouting over her shoulder as she goes.

"Race you to the lighthouse!"

Her hair flies behind her as she runs and I laugh as I follow her.

Keeping my promise, I chase her anywhere, even in Heaven.

The End

To stay up to date on all Tara Sivec news, please join her mailing list:
http://eepurl.com/H4uaf

Made in the USA
Lexington, KY
30 May 2015